*“Are the dogs always so…***welcoming** *to strangers?”*

“Oh, no. Only men. Especially men in suits. They just love men in suits.”

Her eyes locked on to his shoes, then his trousers, and she shook her head from side to side.

“Maybe that wasn’t the best choice of outfit for rolling about with the hounds, Mr. Castellano.”

Choice! He hadn’t been given any choice at all!

“What makes you think that my name is Castellano? Miss…”

“Mrs. Martinez. Ella Martinez.”

She cocked her head to one side for a moment and gave him a smile that created little dimples in each cheek as though she could read his mind as easily as a book.

“Relax. I’m not a journalist, or a mind reader. Just the housekeeper. This means that I’ve been dusting your photographs on top of the grand piano every week for the past three years.”

She paused, then glanced sideways at the sleek red car blocking the lane. “My little boy loves the pictures with all the pretty ladies from the Monaco Grand Prix. Strange there isn’t one of you sitting on your…best pants, in the grass. Shall I run and find my camera?”

“Pleasure to meet you, Mrs. Martinez, and please call me Seb. As for a camera? Thank you, but no. I am embarrassed enough as it is.”

She chuckled gently before replying. “Don’t be. In fact, …an see you are quite comfortable there, so I’ll meet you …he house whenever you feel like it. Bye for now. …!”

Praise for Nina Harrington

Tipping the Waitress with Diamonds

"Witty, warm-hearted and wonderfully emotional, with this novel Nina Harrington once again balances pathos and humor so deftly that readers will be laughing and crying in equal measures as they get swept away by this tender, believable and heartwarming story."

—*Cataromance.com*

Always the Bridesmaid

"Complex characters with terrific chemistry enhance Harrington's simple plot. It's a delightful effort from a new author to watch."

—*RT Book Reviews*

NINA HARRINGTON

The Last Summer of Being Single

TORONTO • NEW YORK • LONDON
AMSTERDAM • PARIS • SYDNEY • HAMBURG
STOCKHOLM • ATHENS • TOKYO • MILAN • MADRID
PRAGUE • WARSAW • BUDAPEST • AUCKLAND

ISBN-13: 978-0-373-17720-2

THE LAST SUMMER OF BEING SINGLE

First North American Publication 2011

This edition published by arrangement with Harlequin Books S.A.

For questions and comments about the quality of this book please contact us at Customer_eCare@Harlequin.ca.

www.eHarlequin.com

Printed in U.S.A.

Nina Harrington grew up in rural Northumberland, England, and decided at the age of eleven that she was going to be a librarian—because then she could read *all* the books in the public library whenever she wanted! Since then she has been a shop assistant, community pharmacist, technical writer, university lecturer, volcano walker and industrial scientist, before taking a career break to realize her dream of being a fiction writer. When she is not creating stories that make her readers smile, her hobbies are cooking, eating, enjoying good wine—and talking, for which she has had specialist training.

To my wonderful editor Jenny Hutton, for her unfailing passion for the genre and commitment to creating the best story possible for our readers. We make a great team. Thank you, Jenny.

CHAPTER ONE

'MARRY me. Come on. You know you want to!'

Ella Jayne Bailey Martinez tapped her finger on her lower lip and nodded her head several times as though trying to make up her mind.

Unfortunately Henri took this as an encouraging sign.

'I have my own set of wheels. You'll be able to motor anywhere you like in this town. What do you say, cutie? We could make some sweet music together!'

'Well… It is tempting. Although…Mr Dubois has already promised me the use of his senior citizen travel card. And it's hard to turn down that sort of offer.'

'Dubois? All promises. No action. Not like me, baby,' Henri replied with a saucy wink.

'Um. That's what I'm worried about. I'm a one-guy-at-a-time kind of girl, and I saw you two-timing me last night with the hotel receptionist. You handsome heartbreaker! Catch you later!'

Henri slammed his hand down hard on the arm of his wheelchair and muttered a vague expletive in French before shrugging his shoulders at Ella and replying in English.

'Darn! Busted!'

Ella smiled and ruffled up what was left of his hair, before sashaying slowly down the corridor back to the kitchen. Without looking back, as though she knew that Henri was still following her every movement, Ella broke step, gave two exaggerated tight bottom wiggles, then glanced back at the grey-haired Romeo just as he winked at her with a twist of the head. 'That's my girl!'

And with a nodding smile Henri swung his wheelchair around with a rim twirl, and sped off at a surprising turn of speed towards the conservatory dining room, where a peal of raucous laughter echoed around the walls as the automatic doors slid open, then closed behind him.

'I hope my guests are not making life too exhausting for you!'

Ella grinned back at her friend Sandrine, who managed the small hotel where she worked as cocktail pianist whenever she could—and occasionally helped out at lunchtimes.

'They're the best! I could talk to them all day about old-style jazz. I grew up with that sort of music. Did you know that Henri spent three years in New Orleans? *And* his pals have just wolfed down three of my apple tarts! Musicians are the same wherever you go in the world! Food comes a close second to the tune! Even in France.'

Sandrine wrapped one arm around Ella's shoulder and grinned. 'Are you kidding? Those charmers might claim that they don't have a sweet tooth in their heads, but once they take a look at the dessert trolley? No will power whatsoever! Thanks again for helping me out at short notice. I have my hands full!'

'No problem. I was glad to help. Are you still fully booked for next weekend?'

'Every room! I've never had forty guests staying for a complete weekend before.'

Sandrine gave Ella an extra hug before releasing her with a warm smile. 'And I know who I have to thank for that! Now don't look so coy. I know that you told Nicole that this was the only hotel you could possibly recommend for all of the guests who are flying in for her birthday party next week. This is true, of course! But thank you all the same.'

'Well, she did ask for my opinion! I'm just so pleased that Nicole decided to celebrate her birthday at the farmhouse instead of staying in Paris. She visits so rarely these days.'

'Isn't that one of the advantages of looking after a holiday home? You get to enjoy a lovely house all to yourself for most of the year while Nicole is in Paris or travelling?'

Ella closed her eyes and grinned contentedly. 'You're right. I love the house and couldn't imagine living anywhere else except the Mas Tournesol. We're so lucky.' Then her eyes flicked open. 'Nicole deserves the best birthday party the old house has ever seen and I'm going to do my best to make sure that she gets it! After all, you are only sixty years young once in your life.'

'Absolutely! And don't forget. You know where to come for anything you need.'

Ella air kissed Sandrine on both cheeks and gave her a swift smile.

'You're a star! But now I'm going to be late for Dan when he gets home from school. See you tomorrow!'

Time to make her escape before Henri finished his afternoon coffee and the caffeine rush inspired him to come up with an even better offer.

'PSN Media have come back with an even better offer but are still dragging their heels on the employee numbers. I'm not sure how far we can push them on the benefits package without impacting the overall deal,' Matt explained, his exasperation clear even down a cell phone.

Sebastien Castellano drummed the fingers of both hands on the leather-covered steering wheel of his low-slung Italian sports car and fought to keep his blood pressure down by focusing on the rows of grapevines that stretched out from his parking spot to the low green hills and shrubby *garrigue* beyond the isolated narrow country road in the middle of the Languedoc.

He had just worked through the night and most of Thursday with Matt and a negotiation team from PSN Media in a stuffy conference room in Montpellier to pull together a deal that could save the jobs of the hundreds of employees who made up Castellano Tech in Australia.

And PSN Media *still* refused to take him seriously!

Yes, they were the premier telecoms company in the field worldwide, but this was his private company. The company he had created from nothing.

He was not going to stand back while PSN Media tried to buy him out with no regard for the welfare of his workforce and their families.

Until recently he had interviewed every single employee himself, and many had been loyal to him from the early days when he risked everything on a crazy idea for a digital media company. His team had built Castellano Tech into the top media company across Australia. And he was not going to let them down for the sake of a few dollars. Loyalty went both ways.

Shame that PSN Media could not see it that way. And unless they were prepared to change their stance, he would not be signing the deal on Monday. The chief executive of PSN Media would have to sail his private yacht out of Montpellier empty-handed.

Seb took a long breath before replying.

'I know you're working hard on this, Matt, but we made our position perfectly clear. PSN Media either guarantees the workforce keep their jobs and the same benefits package for at least the next two years… Or I walk away. No compromise.'

His chief financial officer sighed on the other end of the telephone. 'It could cost you a lot of money, mate.'

Seb sighed out loud. PSN Media thought that every man had a price and that they could buy him off with money. Well, they were badly wrong if they thought that Sebastien Castellano's principles of looking after his staff could be bought, and he was the man who was going to prove it to them.

Seb paused before going on. Matt was only doing his job as Seb's second in command and doing it very well. He had lost just as many hours of sleep as Seb had over the past couple of weeks. They both needed a break.

'A few hours ago we told PSN Media that they had the weekend to come up with their final offer. Sorry, Matt, but nothing has changed during the time it has taken me to drive to the Languedoc. End of story.'

'As stubborn as ever!' Matt replied with a snort. 'Let me make the call. *Then* I suggest we both take time to do something different. Sleep might be nice, for example.'

'Best idea I've heard all day!' Seb added, trying to bring a lighter tone to his voice. 'Take the rest of the day off and I'll catch up tomorrow.'

'It's a deal! Maybe I'll go and see some of those wild flamingos you were telling me about. And say hello to Nicole for me. She must be thrilled you're in France in time for her birthday. Call you tomorrow!'

The cell phone clicked off, leaving Sebastien sitting silently cocooned in air-conditioned luxury and bristling with anticipation and frustration. This merger with PSN Media was the deal of a lifetime. Within six months the communication systems he had designed with his team in a converted garage in Sydney could be in use around the world!

He was so close to achieving his dream he felt like punching his fist into the air!

Yes. He could have gone global with his own design in

time, but merging with PSN Media was the best and fastest way to roll out his award-winning technology.

After ten years of long days and longer nights he was so close to the biggest deal of his life, he could feel it!

Of course, there had been a heavy price to pay for the punishing workload he had given himself. He had left a series of failed relationships and missed family events behind in Sydney.

But it had been worth it.

A few days from now Castellano Tech could be part of a global company and he would have a seat on the board of directors with new responsibilities and a brilliant business future ahead of him. He would be working from his existing company offices in Sydney—the vibrant and exciting city that had provided him with means and opportunities to put his plans into action.

And he would have the time and money to work on a very special project.

Income from the sale of Castellano Tech would provide him with the finance and the technical resources to fully fund the Helene Castellano Foundation. His pilot schemes all over Australasia had already shown that access to modern technology and communication systems could make a difference in the remotest parts of the world. And he *would* commit the time and resources to make those projects work.

His mother, Helene, would have loved the idea.

He could hardly wait to get back to Sydney and start work. The team was already in place, the plans scoped out—all that was needed was the final green light and a substantial part of the nine-figure sum that PSN Media were paying him for the merger.

But that would have to be fitted into next week's diary.

Today he had a much nicer assignment.

Today he was going to meet up with Nicole Lambert, the

lovely woman who had been his stepmother for twelve tumultuous years before she divorced his father and moved back to Paris from Sydney. He had given her plenty of trouble as a teenager but she had stuck by him and supported his career choice every step of the way—with not much in the way of thanks at the time. Their relationship had only really taken off in the last few years they spent together in Sydney—but he still had a lot of making up to do.

When he'd agreed to start secret negotiations with PSN Media he had not known that the company had made their European headquarters in the south of France and the city of Montpellier—and within driving distance from the old Castellano family house in the Languedoc where Nicole had arranged to hold her sixtieth birthday party.

For the first time in years, they would be in the same country within travelling distance at the same time.

Thinking back, he had to agree it was going to be a first.

He had barely managed to make it to her fiftieth birthday in Sydney after a major satellite disaster during a telecoms launch in Japan. Christmas and other family celebrations were out of the question, even before she divorced his father. So the fact that he was actually willing and able to attend her birthday party was something new.

Perhaps that was why he felt totally guilty about the fact that he was going to miss the party after all.

Nicole had been so delighted when he accepted her party invitation that she had insisted that he stay at the Castellano farmhouse rather than a grand hotel.

Of course, Nicole had not accused him directly of having his own agenda, but she must have suspected that something else was going on and he regretted not being able to tell her the truth about the business negotiations, especially when the meeting was brought forward a full week by PSN Media to coincide with the arrival of their CEO.

Which meant that if the deal went through as he hoped, a week from now he would be back in Sydney with a new job and a full workload. And not in the Languedoc helping Nicole to celebrate her birthday. But at least he could spend the weekend with her. That was *something*, even if he had to keep his cell phone turned on and be prepared to drive back to Matt at a moment's notice.

It was time to go and tell Nicole the bad news and apologise for missing her birthday. If he was lucky, she might forgive him. Yet again.

Free at last!

Ella pedalled a little faster for a few minutes to build up extra speed on the straight section of empty country road, then leant back on her bicycle saddle, stretched out both legs either side of the front wheel and lifted up her head to face the brilliant sunshine of an early July afternoon in the Languedoc.

The soft breeze cooled her bare arms and lower legs, and she could almost taste the salt from the Mediterranean only a few miles away to the south. The combination of sunshine and breeze was heavenly and she breathed a blissful sigh of sensual delight.

The familiar stillness and calm of the surrounding countryside acted like a stimulant to her tired head. Sandrine had called just after eight that morning to ask if she could come in to help serve lunch to a party of American jazz enthusiasts who were spending the weekend at the jazz festival in a nearby town.

How she wished she could go with them to the festival! It would be wonderful to spend time revelling in the thrill and excitement of the music she had grown up with—the music she had loved to sing and play professionally since she was sixteen. The music her parents still played for a living. Sometimes she missed her old life so much it hurt to think about it. It was easier to block it out of her mind and focus on the joy of living in this lovely place. Dan had to come first. He was all that mattered now.

The downside of being a housekeeper was that occasionally the owner of the house she loved actually wanted to live in it! Nicole was lovely, kind and generous and had given her a home and a job when she needed it most. For that alone she was prepared to work harder than ever to make sure that Nicole's sixtieth birthday party was a brilliant success. For the first time since they moved here, the house was going to be alive and bursting with fun and laughter! Wonderful.

And then Nicole would be gone for a week or two before returning for the traditional August holiday break. Leaving Ella to spend precious school holidays having fun with Dan.

A warm grin cracked her face and she took a moment to take in the orderly rows of trained grapevines that fanned out from the road towards the low pine-clad hills on one side and the sea on the other. Birdsong and the rustle of the plane trees on the side of the road filled her ears. With the extra flapping of a tiny flag that Dan had fastened with half a roll of tape to the side of his cycle seat.

The simple pleasures of a six-year-old. That simple pennant fluttering in the breeze as they whipped along gave him such pure joy it would have been churlish to point out that it was a Spanish flag from his grandparents and not perhaps the most politically correct item for the south of France. No matter.

This part of the Languedoc was not like Nice or Marseilles. There were no bright city lights, busy city streets or trendy bars or four-star restaurants. This was the working rural farmland that made France so very special. Even the tourist season was short here, and local small hotels like Sandrine's were only truly busy between May and October when visitors flocked into the area to enjoy the wonderful beaches and small villages in the Carmargue or east to Provence.

She wanted, needed, more time with Dan. He was growing up so fast. And now she was his only parent her little boy needed her so badly it broke her heart to leave him in the evenings so that she could bring in some much-needed extra cash working as a cocktail pianist in Sandrine's hotel. Of course he had the best babysitters in France catering to his every need, and it was only for special parties like this one, but she loved their time together in the evenings, especially when the weather was warm enough to sit outside with the dogs.

Only one more day to the summer school holidays! Fantastic.

A prickle of apprehension went through her and she shivered despite the warm breeze. The school holidays meant something else. Something she did not want to think about. Dan would be spending two weeks with his grandparents in Barcelona. The same grandparents who had fought so hard to take control of Dan away from her after his father died—and almost succeeded.

Oh, Christobal! You would have loved how your little boy has turned out!

She only had to look into Dan's eyes to see the man she had loved and married in a whirlwind smile back at her. And nobody was ever going to threaten to take Dan away from her again. She was going to make sure of that.

Even though it had meant saying goodbye to her professional musical career.

The road lifted in a small rise and as she dropped her feet back into the pedals the call of the local seabirds brought her back to the real world and the fact that school would be closing for the day in under an hour. Time to get pedalling!

Seb slipped out from the cool interior of his car to stand on the grass verge in the warm sunshine.

Facing him on the other side of the two-lane tarmac road were the narrow gateposts of the Mas Tournesol. The Languedoc farmhouse where he had been born and spent the first twelve years of his life.

It seemed a very long time ago.

Which probably explained why he didn't remember it being so narrow or overgrown, but perhaps his perspective was different as a boy of twelve from a man of thirty?

Back then there had been two matching heavy wrought-iron gates with the name of the farmhouse picked out in metal. *Mas Tournesol. The Sunflower House.*

Now one of the gates had been knocked off its hinges and was lying in the gravel and grass on the side of the path with weeds growing up between the filigree metal. The gate must have been lying there for months. There was no sign of its partner.

Memories of a childhood playing in these fields told him that there was a rippling river on the other side of the straight row of rustling shady plane trees to his left where he had spent many happy hours fishing with his dad. The hedges on the right formed the boundary to the vineyards and sunflower fields his dad had sold to their neighbour only days before they emigrated, but the branches were taller now, choked with bushes and flowering shrubs.

A rush of sadness swept over him as he thought of the last time he had travelled down this lane on his way to a new life and his breath came out of his lungs in a juddering rattle.

Perhaps he wasn't as prepared for this as he thought he was?

Closing his eyes for a second, he saw his mother's flower garden again in his mind's eye, and walked along its winding paths, their heady scent filling the air against the buzz of honey bees and birdsong. And for a few moments he was transported back to that one place on this earth that would always be embedded deep inside and to the happiest period of time in his life.

Before his mother died.

Seb slowly opened his eyes into the glare from the sun and adjusted his designer sunglasses.

He had resisted coming back to this house for so many reasons. He might have lived in Sydney since the age of twelve and adored his life there, but he was still a Frenchman with his heart rooted in a deep heritage of land and culture. That could not be denied.

But something else drew him here. And the feeling unsettled him. At first he had put it down to anxiety about the business deal, but it was more than that. It was a strange sense of dissatisfaction and nagging unease that he had managed to push under the surface of his life for the past six months.

In fact, ever since he found out that his dad could not be his natural father.

Yes, he had been shocked by the surprise of it. Yes, he was astonished and taken aback, but he had not allowed the earthquake of the revelation to shake his world to pieces. He had grown up in a loving family with two caring parents and travelling the world on his charity projects had shown him just how precious a thing that was to a child.

No matter what the truth of his birth, he was proud of his mother and always would be. She had put him first. Only… he could not help but wonder why she had not told him the truth. Especially at the end when they all knew that time was short and he had spent many hours alone with her while she was still lucid. *Just talking.* And she had kept her secret.

Of course these past months had been filled with frenetic activity in the business. This was his first opportunity to take a real break, even if it was just a few hours in between discussions with Matt or the PSN Media legal team.

It made sense to spend a few days with Nicole and put his mind at ease.

Seb raised his shoulders up towards his ears, then dropped them back down to help relieve the tension. He needed *something* to put his mind at ease!

Because now he was back where he started!

Back to the house that now belonged to his former stepmother, Nicole, who won this house in the divorce from his dad.

It was hers to do with as she liked, even if that meant only using it as a holiday house for a few weeks a year. Or as a venue for her birthday party.

Nicole probably didn't even realise that this was the same week as the anniversary of his mother's death. And that his precious mother had taken her last breath in this house.

Seb pushed back his shoulders and lifted his head higher.

He knew one thing.

He would never again allow himself to love one person and one place so completely. Not when they could be snatched away from him at a moment's notice and he was powerless to prevent it. Especially knowing what he knew now.

He didn't believe in focusing on the past—only the future. And that meant honouring his mother through the charity work that was changing lives *now*. His old life was gone. Over. And the sooner he got back to Sydney and started on the new projects, the better.

He was here to spend the weekend with Nicole, catch up with his emails, then get back to the negotiating table first thing Monday morning before flying home. And that was all. The sooner the better.

A few minutes later Sebastien gingerly edged his rented very wide, very red and very shiny Italian sports car between the posts and started slowly down the gravel path, which was becoming more and more familiar by the metre.

A splash of frustration at his own inability to control his anxiety and apprehension for this stretch of rough roadway hit Seb hard and fast as cold as the air conditioning and he straightened his back and revved up the engine, oblivious to the flying gravel on the paintwork and thrilling to the glorious roar from under the bonnet.

He only hoped the gardens would not be as overgrown as the driveway, but he would find out soon enough. Once around the next blind corner, he would be able to see the rooftops of the house.

He had been a fool to come here and expect the place to be the same.

The car picked up a little speed as he reached the corner, his eyes focused on the skyline looking for the house.

And then he suddenly slammed the brakes on so hard that the antilock brakes on the car activated and he came to a screeching halt on the loose gravel.

Something was lying in the road. Looking at him.

CHAPTER TWO

HEART thumping, it took a few seconds for Sebastien to catch his breath and unclamp his fingers from the steering wheel.

Knuckles still white, he flung open the car door, stretched his long legs out of the bucket seat and onto the path, the full heat of the afternoon sunshine hot on the back of his neck.

Laid out across the middle of the road only a few inches from the front of his car was a large grey and dapple brown dog who clearly had no intention of moving. Anywhere.

The dog was lying with its head on his paws, his shaggy coat thick with dust from the road and an extra layer of gravel that had been scattered by the car's sudden stop.

And it was not just any dog. It was a hunting griffon, just like the one the kids on the next farm used to have when he was a boy. There was no mistaking the whiskers and heavy grey eyebrows on an old bearded face. He had not seen a griffon for years and just the sight of those intelligent eyes looking up at him made Seb smile as he stepped closer to check the dog was not injured.

Seb breathed a sigh of relief and hunkered down onto the back of his heels to take a closer look at this strange beast, who simply pushed a brown nose into Seb's outstretched hand and sniffed heavily through wide open-flared nostrils before yawning widely, displaying a good set of teeth.

'Not the best place to choose to have a nap, old mate,' Seb

muttered as the griffon wagged his tail, then turned on his side to have his tummy tickled, completely unharmed and apparently oblivious to the heart attack he had almost given the driver of the car who had come close to running him over.

The dog clearly liked what he smelt because Seb's hand was given an experimental couple of licks before the ears twitched and the intelligent yellow eyes below the hairy eyebrows looked up into his face.

Then suddenly the griffon's head shot up and both ears lifted as he pushed himself into a sitting position.

'What is it, boy? What have you heard?' Seb asked in French, but before the dog could bark a reply a gaggle of energy and four legs burst through the bushes and undergrowth and leapt up, barking loudly, and struck Seb straight in the chest with enough force to send him flying backwards from the gravel path into the thick grass. And briars. And nettles. And whatever other bio matter the local wildlife had left there since it was last cut.

It took a few seconds for Seb to gather his wits and raise both of his hands to fend off the attack from a very wet tongue and even wetter fur ball, but it was too late to block the pair of wet muddy front paws dancing and prancing with delight on the front of Seb's couture south sea island cotton business shirt. He didn't want to think about his suit trousers. Not yet. From this angle the monster looked like a younger version of the dog on the path. The dog equivalent to a hyperactive toddler high on additives and sugar.

The grin and tail wagging said it all.

This was dog language for: *Look what I've found! Someone new to play with! This is fun! Shall we see what tricks it can do?*

Its older friend or relative decided that guarding the path was boring and took to hunting in the bushes.

Okay. Time to move.

Seb pushed himself up on one elbow and was immediately pounced on by the young hound, who had found a piece of stick for him to throw, his paws diving back and forward for attention.

Seb stared at it for a moment before chuckling out loud to himself.

This was turning out to be quite a day! Being knocked over by a playful puppy was nothing compared to a very long flight followed by two days of hard business negotiations and a short drive in a strange car on French roads he had last seen eighteen years earlier.

With a sigh he turned to the hopeful hound that was still prancing with his throwing stick and waved him away with one hand before speaking.

'Not a chance, fella. Let me get back on my feet first.'

Only he never got the chance since the dog suddenly dropped the stick and took off at great speed back down the lane towards the main road, leaving Seb alone with the older dog, who was shuffling towards him for an ear rub.

'Just you and me, mate? Where do you live? Um?'

'Milou doesn't speak English. And he lives with me, Mr Castellano.'

It was a woman's voice. Her words were spoken in perfect English with the same type of accent he had heard many times from his British colleagues at the Castellano Tech headquarters back in Sydney. This particular bodiless voice was coming from the part of the lane he had just driven down so that its owner was hidden out of view behind his car.

Great! The first person he met in his old home village and he was flat on the back in the grass. And he had already been recognised. So much for wanting to keep a low profile!

He wondered how long she had been there watching him.

Seb sighed out loud and shook his head at just how

ridiculous he must look at that moment. He had two choices. Start yelling about out-of-control hounds off the leash, which would hardly be fair considering that this was a private road in the middle of the countryside, or smile and move on.

By pushing himself up with one hand in a spot with the least number of stinging nettles, Seb managed to get himself to a sitting position without looking too much like an idiot, before paying more attention to the woman—who clearly knew who he was.

'Hello! Are these your dogs? They're quite a handful,' he asked in English.

A pair of straw-coloured espadrille shoes on the ends of slim tanned female legs appeared in the space between the gravel and the bottom of his sports car, then walked slowly around the front so that they were standing directly in front of him.

The ankle within touching distance wore a thin ankle bracelet with tiny ceramic flowers—but the lace in this shoe was green while the lace in the other was stripy blue.

Suddenly more than a little curious about what the rest of the outfit might look like, Seb tried not to ogle as he lifted his gaze up at a yellow and white sundress with thin straps, which hung from tiny collarbones to fall above dark green cut-off Capri pants.

The last time he had seen an outfit like that was at a Christmas charity concert his company has sponsored at a local primary school in Sydney.

He was looking at Peter Pan. Or perhaps it was Tinker Bell?

Lifting his sunglasses with one hand, he risked looking into her face and a pair of shockingly pale blue eyes smiled down at him above a button nose and bow lips.

Her straight light brown hair was tied back from a smooth

forehead with a broad green headband the same colour as her trousers.

He changed his opinion. Peter Pan was never this pretty, or petite. She was tiny! Tinker Bell.

And for a moment his voice did not seem to work as she took one more extra look at him without the slightest bit of concern, then turned to play with the dogs, who had clearly learnt not to jump up on the hand that fed them.

'Hello, gang!' she said in French. 'How are you doing? Sorry that I'm so late! Have you missed me?'

Her knuckles rubbed each of the dogs in turn, and then she flung the stick down the road away from the car—'Go on. Meet you back at the house!' Then stood back and smiled as they raced away.

Only then did this lovely apparition smile down at Seb and switch back into English.

'Don't worry. You can play with them later!'

Play. He had no intention of *playing* with them! Seb sighed out loud and shook his head. Her cheery tone was too infectious for him to be angry with her for the ridiculous position he was in.

'Are they always so…*welcoming* to strangers?'

'Oh, no. Only men. Especially men in suits. They just love men in suits.'

Her eyes locked onto his shoes then his trousers and she shook her head from side to side.

'On the other hand you are never going to get the stains out of those trousers. Maybe that wasn't the best choice of outfit for rolling about with the hounds!'

Choice! He hadn't been given any choice at all!

'Do you need some help with the car, Mr Castellano? We don't have a garage but I've cleared a space in the barn for you to use during your stay. There is a mistral forecast.'

Staying? How did she know that? Maybe there was more to this girl.

'What makes you think that my name is Castellano? Miss…'

'Mrs Martinez. Ella Martinez.'

She cocked her head to one side for a moment and gave him a smile that created little dimples in each cheek as though she could read his mind as easily as a book.

'Relax. I'm not a journalist, or a mind-reader. Just Nicole's housekeeper. This means that I've been dusting your photographs on top of the grand piano every week for the past three years.'

She paused, then glanced sideways at the sleek red car blocking the lane. 'My little boy loves the pictures with all of the pretty ladies from the Monaco Grand Prix, but Nicole prefers the yacht racing. Strange she doesn't have one of you sitting on your…best pants, in the grass. Shall I run and find my camera?'

Seb dropped his head towards one shoulder before snorting out a reply. Nicole had a housekeeper! That made sense.

'Pleasure to meet you, Mrs Martinez, and please call me Seb. As for a camera? Thank you, but no. In fact I am highly relieved that you do *not* have a camera. I am embarrassed enough as it is.'

She chuckled gently before replying.

'Don't be. In fact I can see you are quite comfortable there,' Ella replied with a small bow. 'So I'll meet you back at the house whenever you feel like it. Your room is all ready for you. Bye for now. And it's Ella!'

With one small finger wave she strolled back behind his car and pulled a very strange-looking ancient bicycle with a child seat through the bushes, gracefully pushed off with one foot on the pedal and calmly cycled down the lane towards the house, leaving him sitting there surrounded by birdsong, the buzz of insects, dogs barking somewhere close and the ping, ping, ping of condensation dripping onto hot metal from the air conditioning in the car.

He watched in silence as a yellow butterfly landed on his outstretched hand, cleaned its feelers, and then lifted away.

'Well, you are a long way from Kansas now, Toto,' he mumbled before chuckling to himself, then chuckling louder, the ridiculous nature of his position hitting him right in the funny bone.

So much for the millions in his private bank accounts! Thank heavens the 'suits' at PSN Media could not see him now! They might think twice about buying a company from a farm boy.

This was turning out to be quite a day! And he had only just arrived.

It was almost a shame that he would not be staying long enough to find out more about Nicole's housekeeper!

A few minutes later, Seb stepped out from the car and felt the small hairs at the back of his neck stand on end.

The outside of the house had not changed that much in eighteen years. The farmhouse had been built from sandstone, which he already knew took on a golden-pink hue at dusk in the long summer evenings. The long wooden shutters that covered the windows and patio doors used to be painted a lavender-blue shade that he had never seen anywhere else except in this part of the Languedoc. Now they were dark blue with a pale yellow trim, which to his untrained eye was too harsh a colour contrast below the old terracotta tile roof spotted with patches of moss.

Any fears he might have had about his old home being a ruin were gone, replaced by a general sense of unease that brought a crease of tension to his forehead and a strange quiver of anxious fear in his gut matched with a cold sweat in the small of his back, despite the warmth of his shirt and suit jacket.

He had not expected to feel this way.

He had formed his own company, which had grown into an international multimillion-dollar business, he thought nothing of giving presentations to hundreds of strangers and yet here he was, standing in the warm sunshine, and nervous of taking those few steps through the tall and, oh, so familiar wooden door that led inside the house where he had grown up.

Suddenly a light breeze picked up through the resin-heavy poplar and plane trees and carried the scent of lavender, roses, honeysuckle and sweet white jasmine. Instantly his mind was flooded with so many memories that he sucked in a breath to help steady himself.

Thousands of moments and images that all called out the same message.

You've come home.

After almost a lifetime away from the country of his birth, this area, this village and this farmhouse…he was home.

And the very thought shocked him more than he thought possible.

Home was the apartment in Sydney with the stunning views over the city where he slept some of the time and kept his clothes. Sydney was his home. Not here. Not any more.

He had decided eighteen years ago that he would never again rely so much on one person for his happiness. The agony of being dragged away from this house had destroyed that kind of childish sentimentality for good.

He did not do sentimental.

Indeed the notion shocked him so much that when Ella sauntered around the side of the house and stood next to him looking up at the window, he barely noticed her presence until her light sweet voice broke the silence.

'Has it changed much since you were here last?'

He half turned and blinked in confusion as he fought to regain the connection between his brain and his mouth. *Had she been reading his mind?*

She tilted her chin upward and looked at him eye to eye. 'Nicole told me that you grew up here. I was just wondering if the house is still the same as you remember. That's all!' And with that she turned away to pick off dead flower heads from the cascades of stunning blossoms billowing from two giant stone urns that stood either side of the main door, giving Seb a chance to put together a sensible reply.

'Er, no. Not much. I noticed the gates are down—' he sniffed '—but the house itself looks pretty much the same.' He raised one hand toward the shutters with a nod. 'The colour scheme is different. Not sure it works.'

There was an exasperated sigh from Ella who twirled around to face him and planted a fist firmly on each hip.

'Thank you! Nicole hired an "interior designer"—' at this point she lifted her hands and made quotation marks with her fingers '—to remodel the old place in the spring.'

Ella nodded towards the shutters and shuddered with her shoulders. 'He was a lovely charming man who had a wonderful eye for textiles but had *no* clue about the local style. I mean none. Zip. *De nada*. Zero.'

She bent towards Seb as though confiding in him. 'I may be from London but I have lived here long enough to know that this house does not need navy-blue shutters!'

Then she stepped back to the flowers and expertly snipped off a perfect half-open pink rose bud with a few glossy green leaves with a fingernail.

Before Seb could reply she skipped up, stood on tiptoe and slipped the rose into the buttonhole of his made-to-measure suit jacket, smoothing it into place on his soft cashmere collar with the fingertips of one hand.

'There. That's better. No thorns, you see. I planted a rose without thorns. Do you like it?'

Ella raised her brows and looked Seb straight in the eye with an intense look and suddenly her mouth twitched as if she was only too aware that as he looked down to admire the new addition to his wardrobe he had a delightful view down the front of her yellow and white sundress.

For a few moments he completely forgot his troubles as he admired the tanned skin and soft curves under the thin yellow and white cotton. A white lacy bra peeked out either side of the dress, which had slipped down over one shoulder, and he felt the sudden urge to lift the strap of her sundress back into position. But that would have meant touching her skin and finding out if it was truly as soft and smooth as it looked.

It was very tempting but also totally prohibited.

Oh, no. Not going there. Bad idea! He liked city-smart women who knew how to run multimedia servers and could make orbiting satellites obey his commands. Not elves in green pants. Especially when she released her hand from his jacket and he saw a diamond and sapphire wedding band on her left ring finger.

Mrs Martinez! A married housekeeper. Okay. Very prohibited! That made sense. He vaguely recalled that she mentioned a little boy. *A married woman with a family.* The perfect housekeeper and gardener and maintenance man team to look after the house when Nicole was away.

Mr Martinez was a very lucky man.

He brought his attention back onto the trellis of roses above her head before croaking out a reply. 'I do like it. It's a stunning display. Thank you, Mrs Martinez.'

She gave his jacket a small final pat and smiled back at him before dropping back onto her heels.

'You are most welcome. The main rose garden is still at the back of the house.' She paused for a second, then gestured to the car and flashed him a half-smile. Then it was back to business. 'Even in that mobile sofa you call a car, you must be tired after your long drive. Ready to see what he did to your old bedroom?'

This *had* been his room. The ancient bathroom with the cracked enamel basin had been in the room next door. The wall must have been knocked through to create this stylish tiled ensuite. But the room itself had not changed that much and the floorboards certainly creaked in the same places.

The rush of memories threatened to overwhelm him again as he looked out from the square window onto the walled garden at the back of the house where he had played and learnt to love life.

And then it hit him.

Ella Martinez had made up *this* room for him. Not the spare room his grandmother had used when his mother was terminally ill, but *his* old room. How had she known that this had been his room?

He turned back towards the door. Ella was standing at the top of the stairs simply watching him and her smile was like sunshine inside the dark cool shade of the corridor.

Seeing the look on his face, she said, 'I worked it out,' then pointed to the wall behind his back. 'From the wallpaper.'

Then she grinned and took pity on his confusion. 'Relax. I'm not psychic. When the decorators stripped off the layers of wallpaper they found some interesting blasts from the past.'

Ella glanced back over each shoulder, and then peeked down the staircase, as though checking that they were not being overhead, before leaning closer.

'I'm sure lots of teenagers back then plastered their bedroom walls with posters of their favourite pop groups. In fact—' and at this she leant back, pursed her lips, and nodded before going on '—I'm willing to bet that you would sing along to your favourite records holding a hairbrush as a pretend microphone. Am I right?'

Seb felt the back of his neck flare with heat and embarrassment, only then he looked at Ella and the laughter that had been teasing the corner of her mouth bubbled through into a full warm giggle.

Nobody had dared giggle at Sebastien Castellano for a very long time, only there was something in Ella's voice that told him that her comments were not insulting or meant to embarrass him. She was simply sharing a joke.

And suddenly the irony of his old posters being found almost twenty years later hit him hard and he made the mistake of looking back at Ella. He started to laugh, really laugh, the sound so unfamiliar to him that he realised with a rush that he had not laughed like this for a long time.

'Quite wrong,' he eventually managed to reply, wiping the tears from his eyes. 'It wasn't a hairbrush. It was a can of my grandmother's hairspray. And the old wardrobe had a full-length mirror so I could admire my new denim outfit in its full glory.'

'In that case consider yourself lucky. My parents are full-time musicians and I was actually born above their jazz club in London. Can you imagine what the noise was like every evening?' Ella paused and looked up at the ceiling before sighing out loud. 'Actually it was amazing and I adored it.' She shrugged her shoulders. 'Hey ho. On with the show. I'll leave you to get settled. If you need anything I'll be in the same place as the coffee and cookies.'

Seb nodded. 'On with the show? Okay, that sounds good. One question. What time are you expecting Nicole today? I need to catch up with her as soon as she gets back.'

Ella's brows came together and her mouth twisted in surprise. 'Nicole? Nicole isn't here. Didn't she tell you?'

Seb's frown deepened as he looked up at Ella.

'Not here? I don't understand. She emailed me a few weeks ago to make sure that my plans had not changed. Has something happened? Is she okay?'

Ella raised and lowered both hands. 'Fine. As of this morning she is just fine. A little wet maybe, but fine. What is not so fine is the weather in Nepal. The monsoon rains have come early and she is finding it slow going walking back from Everest Base Camp. They've already missed their original flight. So, you see, Nicole won't be back for at least another few days.'

Then she added with a small shoulder shrug, 'Until then you are stuck with me.'

CHAPTER THREE

ELLA peeped out of the kitchen window to see if Seb had woken from his nap yet.

She had hoped that he would be awake in time to move the very fine example of Italian design he called a motor vehicle that was still half parked, half abandoned, on the round driveway at the front of the house, before Dan's schoolteacher tried to squeeze her tiny car through.

Everything in the garden was quiet and tranquil. A normal summer afternoon.

Strange. From what Nicole had told her, Sebastien Castellano was used to living life at top speed. Rushing here and there, always looking for the next project or the next business deal where he could have fun bringing modern communications to a company or even a city! Burning the candle at both ends with his remarkable workload and high-profile fund-raising events.

She had not been joking about the silver-framed photographs on the piano that needed regular dusting and polishing. Nicole had built up quite a collection.

Although there was something odd about the photographs. Something that she had never mentioned out of respect for Nicole's personal life.

The collection did not have one single photo of Sebastien with his father or with Nicole. Not one family picture. Seb wasn't even on Nicole's wedding photo, and he must have been in his late teens when Nicole married Seb's father.

It had always seemed strange. Especially compared to her own personal albums of photos. She treasured the family photos with her parents and Dan. Christobal's family loved formal portraits taken by professionals in a studio, and she was so grateful that she could show Dan what his father had looked like, but she was happy with a spur-of-the-moment shot taken with a cheap pocket camera.

Not for Nicole.

Of course, there was one great advantage in being the person responsible for polishing Sebastien Castellano's face every week. She could allow her imagination to run riot about what the man himself was like in the flesh. Nicole was not the only one thrilled when Sebastien accepted the invitation to her birthday party—out of the blue!

Ella chewed her lower lip. She had hardly believed her eyes when she saw who owned the car blocking the driveway. How could any man look so handsome sitting on his bottom in the hedge playing with Milou and Wolfie?

Although it did make her wonder what he truly was doing here. From what little Nicole had told her, Seb had gone out of his way to *avoid* coming to see her in the past, and he never took a holiday so it was more than a little odd that he turned up like this. Perhaps Nicole was correct and he had his own agenda for being in this part of France?

Ella shook her head with a smile.

Silly girl. Speculating her life away!

It was such a lovely day she could hardly blame Seb for taking time away from work to relax and enjoy the garden of his old home after the long flight from Australia.

While it was time for her to get back to work and for one of her favourite tasks, which Dan adored helping her with. Shelling peas under the trees.

Ella went through the house to the kitchen, picked up her colander and a basket of fresh peas in the pod from the local market, and carried them out to the patio table.

And stopped abruptly, the peas skidding in the basket.

Seb was lying on a recliner with a beaker of now-cold coffee and a home-made cookie from Dan's stash on a tray on the low table next to him.

Fast asleep.

His chest lifted gently up and down under a once crisp formal shirt, now smudged with dog paw marks.

Ella leant as quietly as she could on the edge of the hardwood table and looked at him. *Really* looked at him.

Dappled sunshine flickered over his skin as the light breeze moved through the branches of the trees, lifting the wide leaves to create a mosaic of light and shade on the patio lounger.

The strong handsome face was a road map of luxurious places where the very rich and powerful people liked to visit in their drive to become richer and even more powerful.

Places where sensitive souls like her own would burn up in the intense heat of that fire and driving passion. And from what she could see Sebastien Castellano was at best a little scorched and at worst exhausted from fighting back the flames.

His dark brown eyebrows were thick, wide and set into a powerful broad brow, which had been designed by nature to make his look fierce and intense even when asleep on the lounger.

His dark brown hair was expertly cut into a formal business look—but just a little longer than the average, leaving dark strands falling across his brow and collar.

He had a strong nose, and as she peered closer a sprinkle of sun-kissed freckles made her smile. Probably from his days spent yacht racing in the tropics. Or scuba-diving trips to the

Great Barrier Reef. Something like that. Nothing as mundane as shelling peas in a farmhouse in the Languedoc.

A five o'clock shadow of dark brown stubble stretching down from his sideburns and across his upper lip softened the fierce-looking square jaw, which could have belonged to a prize fighter or matador, rather than a self-made entrepreneur.

His bottom lip was narrow compared to a sumptuous upper lip that photographers loved to capture at prestigious award dinners or business functions.

She could not resist a small sigh. *Oh, how she envied him his lifestyle!* She had loved her old life on the road! Travelling with her parents from town to town, playing jazz and classical concerts wherever they could. She had lost count of the number of weddings, birthdays, festivals and fairs where the Bailey trio had shared their passion for music.

She had spent so many years on the road since she turned sixteen the countries that they visited sometimes blended into one. Spain and Portugal had been amazing, but it was the three months they spent in southern India that she remembered the most. The colours, the energy, the dusty roads that choked you just before you had to sing for two hours! She remembered every minute. And was grateful that she had those memories to look back on.

That life was very far from this safe farmhouse where she could give Dan the benefits of a settled life.

Yes. *You are a very lucky man, Seb Castellano.*

Only at that moment Seb's mouth moved in a charming little twitching action at the side and it hit her hard that Dan did exactly the same thing when he dozed off sometimes.

Ella smiled to herself.

Not exactly the image of the intimidating power-hungry master of Castellano Tech that Nicole kept cuttings about from business magazines!

So this was Nicole's celebrity stepson! Or was that infamous?

He had reacted so oddly when he found out that Nicole was not going to be back until Monday at the earliest. From what Nicole had told her, they were not close and never had been, but he did seem genuinely concerned that she had been delayed.

What was it that he wanted from her friend and employer that he could not ask over the phone, or in an email? What was he here for?

Whatever the reasons, this real live version of Sebastien Castellano looked as though he needed a good meal followed by decent sleep in a soft bed.

Failing that, a power nap in a warm garden would do him good.

Which meant two things; first she had to head off attacks from both the dogs who had disappeared once they had been fed, and her son who should be arriving home from school at any minute.

Turning carefully on the balls of her feet, Ella lifted her basket of peas as quietly as she could—and almost dropped them when Seb's cell phone started ringing.

He stirred twice, sighed loudly, and sat up, quickly grasping onto the cell phone, flicking it open and saying, Yes, before his eyes had even come into focus.

The image was of someone living on a knife edge and suddenly her envy was replaced with pity.

The familiar ring tone broke the deep sleep Seb had been enjoying and he yawned widely and uncreaked his neck muscles as he checked the caller identity and blinked a few times.

'Matt? How are you doing? Oh. Insect bites? Ah, yes. The infamous Camargue mosquito. Should have warned you about those. Sorry, mate.' He chuckled briefly with a closed mouth before getting back to business. 'I take it you've had a call from PSN Media?'

Seb's left hand rubbed vigorously along the line of his powerful jaw and the longer-than-normal designer stubble, then his mouth curved into a knowing smile. 'I knew they would come around on the employee benefits in the end. You've done a great job, Matt. What's that? His private yacht? Trying to impress us, is he? Interesting.'

His hand lifted, then dropped onto his knee. 'If Frank Smith wants to fly a corporate lawyer down from Paris on Monday morning so that we can sign the contract on his yacht, then I'm happy to turn up and enjoy his hospitality—providing the numbers add up.'

Then a sniff. 'Right. In that case, we'll go through the fine print Sunday evening before dinner. Close the deal Monday. Thanks. You too.'

The fingers of both hands clenched hard into his palms as his brain reeled with the implications of the news.

Yes! PSN Media had come up with a compromise on the benefits package. And the chief executive of PSN Media was remarkably choosy when it came to inviting people onto his private yacht. This was a first. It was actually going to happen!

And he knew exactly who to share it with.

In an instant he swiped his finger across the touch screen on his top-of-the-range cell phone, found the contact number he was looking for, and the call was answered in his Sydney office within three rings.

'Hi, Vicky. Seb. It's good news. You've got the green light to start planning the phase two Foundation projects.'

Seb smiled at the shriek of delight and laughter that burst out from the talented project manager he had hired to look after the Helene Castellano Foundation.

'Thought you'd like that. I'll be back in the office next

Wednesday and want to see the projected timelines and budgets some time before Friday's meeting. Think you can manage that? Thought so. What else are weekends for, right? Thanks, Vicky. You too. Yes, it is brilliant news.'

Seb closed his eyes, shook his head with a relaxed grin, then stretched out the length of his body on the lounger like a cat waking from a long sleep, with both arms behind his head.

Vicky was the best in the business and one of the most passionate and enthusiastic people he had ever met. She had chosen to spend her retirement making best use of the contacts she had made during forty years in investment banking. This time next week she would have a dream budget to work with and Seb could get on with the hands-on work implementing the communication systems.

All he had to do was ensure that the offer on the table was signed with no last-minute problems.

Then he would really feel like celebrating. It might be winter back in Sydney but he didn't see any reason why he could not take his team down to the beach for the day! They had worked for this just as hard as he had. They deserved a decent party before the real hard work kicked in. He could not wait to get back to Sydney and get the ball rolling!

He allowed himself a smile.

Then spun around, suddenly conscious that he was not alone, and for a few seconds he had to work out where he was. Then his fists clenched in anger at the intrusion into his private business and thoughts.

He had let his guard down for a moment. Stupid!

Ella recoiled for a second with Seb's sudden movement. A handful of pea pods fell onto the patio stones and she leant down to scoop them up.

Only as she did so Ella recognised that three things had become quite apparent.

Two of them were attached to her chest and she was pointing them quite brazenly under strained cotton and a low-cut sundress at the man whose eyes were now at the same height as her own.

Idiot! She was not used to having men around the house. She really had to think about her clothing for the next week if she wanted to avoid this happening again.

And then came number three. Sebastien Castellano was looking at her.

Amber eyes the colour of beech trees in autumn met hers, flashed with startled energy and widened slightly in surprise that he was being observed so closely. And then those eyes seemed to warm as though melting in the summer heat.

Suddenly she understood what the fuss in the gossip columns was all about.

His eyes were not just amber, they were the deepest dark caramel brown flecked with gold, with a dark centre that pulled you in, like a pool of deep, deep water so dark she would be scared to dive into it for fear of never reaching the bottom. Or of never being able to swim back to the surface.

She had seen a tiny glimpse of that look when he had looked down the front of her dress earlier—which had been completely her own fault. And he had been gentleman enough to look away as soon as he could. But now she was taking in the full blast and the depth and intensity were only too clear.

Ella could feel the beat of her heart in her neck and wrist respond to the power of something very primal that came from a very masculine man who had started to relax once the tension of answering the call had ebbed away, warm and stretching sensuously in the sunshine only inches away from her.

He didn't say anything, or move from his recliner, he simply turned his head and looked back at her. The moment stretched until she could feel it like an elastic band pulled tighter and tighter until she was frightened about what would happen when all of that energy was released.

Heart racing, she opened her mouth to speak but didn't get the chance, because in that fraction of a second doors started slamming all over the house, a car crunched away on the gravel drive and a distinctive voice called out in the local French dialect, 'Mum-m-m! Milou got out again!'

Seb stared at the dog-shaped apparition that joggled towards him to make sure that he was not still dreaming, and blinked hard a couple of times.

Nope. He was awake.

The child's voice had emerged from behind the huge armful of dog that had grown tired of being carried, and the bundle of fur and paws had now decided to come alive and was struggling like a wild thing to be free now he was home.

The child made it as far as the table before he released the furry creature that dropped into a heap of low woof and flying fur and dust onto the patio tiles.

Seb wasn't dreaming after all. And the creature looked remarkably like the old griffon hound that had almost ended up under his tyres on the path.

The cherub of a dark curly-haired boy who emerged tried to brush some of the dog hair from his school shirt, looked at the mess and claw marks, then looked up in astonishment as he realised that there was a strange man lounging on one of the recliners.

'Daniel Charles Bailey Martinez. You. Have not been doing your job.' Ella was bending forward now, her head tilted to one side as she spoke to her son.

The child looked up from the dog towards Sebastien, and

then back to his mother, shrugged and turned around, dropping his shoulders.

'Sorry, Mum.'

'Don't apologise to me, young man. He made it as far as the traffic this time. If Mr Castellano here didn't have good brakes on his car, your old pal Milou might have been injured, and you—' she was pointing now '—you would have to explain how Milou came to be taking a nap in the middle of the road. And that would be. Serious. So, you know what to do.'

She gestured with her head over one shoulder towards Seb, and nodded.

The cherub moved slowly forward with his head down, sidled one step at a time until he was standing in front of Seb, shuffling from side to side, his hands stuffed deep into the pockets of his school trousers.

'Thanks for not killing Milou.'

Seb looked at the little boy's head, then at the dog lying on his back at his feet, waiting to have his tummy tickled. Seb was so used to people around him showing due deference he was not accustomed to a child's version of an apology. He quickly recovered as best he could and replied with a, 'No problem,' in English, before wondering how that translated to child talk.

The child glanced up and whispered in an excited voice, 'Did you have to screech your car? I mean, did you have to skid and everything?'

'Dan!'

His head dropped again.

'I was just asking!'

Dan glanced up at Seb and gave him a toothy smile, which would be breaking hearts in the very near future. It was a signal between boys.

'Matter of fact I did have to screech my tyres. Grit was

flying everywhere. It was like being in one of those rally cars. Even had to skid a bit along the grass.'

'Cool!'

'Oh, I give up. Boys!' Ella turned back to her peas while Milou chose that moment to issue a loud yawn and settled down to sleep after his exciting adventure.

Dan sidled up closer to Sebastien and looked once at Ella, who gave him one single nod before asking in a low whisper, 'Is that *your* car outside? It's the biggest I've *ever seen*.'

Seb bent down from the waist so that he was at the same level as Dan. Interesting. Apparently he had just been given security clearance from Ella.

'Yes, it is my car, but your mother is right, mate.' Seb shook his head. 'I would have felt just awful if I had hurt your dog. I only just managed to turn away in time. Were you supposed to be making sure he didn't make it to the road?'

There was a nod but, from the way the boy's bottom lip was quivering, Seb took the initiative and moved to a different question. He was not used to children at the best of times and he certainly didn't have the training to handle tears.

'Tell me about the other dog. The younger one. Where does he live?'

The little boy glanced back towards Ella and Milou, twisted his mouth from side to side, made a decision, and replied in a big gush, 'Milou is really old now, but Wolfie is a puppy and lives next door at the farm and comes to see us sometimes. Want to see where Wolfie gets through the fence?'

Dan's eyes brightened and he clutched at Seb's sleeve. 'Maybe you can help fix the fence? That way Milou won't squeeze out in the gap? Can you? Can you fix it? Please?'

'Dan! Please don't pester Mr Castellano,' Ella whispered in a kind voice, but Dan had taken firm hold of Seb's sleeve and clearly needed a reply.

Seeing as a working knowledge of hand tools and do-it-yourself carpentry were not skills that Seb considered priorities in software and communication systems design, he decided that mending fence panels was not a job he was qualified to undertake. Besides, Mr Ella Martinez would probably be back from his day job or whatever other task took him away from home on a Thursday afternoon, and could no doubt do a far better job.

So he replied with the first thing that came into his head.

'Why not wait for your dad to come home and then you can fix the fence together? I'm sure he'll do a far better job than I can.'

There was a sudden intake of breath from the tiny brunette sitting at the table, and as Seb glanced up her hands had stilled over the peas and her lips were pressed tight together as she stared intensely into the basket.

This was not a good sign.

Then Dan was shaking his head at him and tugging at his sleeve more urgently, demanding his attention.

'My daddy is in heaven! And Milou is very naughty! Aunty Nicole is having a party. And there are going to be lots of cars and vans and things and that means…*big trouble*.'

Dan sighed twice between these two final words and released Seb to lift both hands in the air.

Seb paused for a second in appreciation of the simple, devastatingly logical thinking of a small boy. Whose daddy was in heaven. And whose fence was broken, and probably had been broken for quite some time.

Perhaps he could apply the same simple childlike logic to the simple request for help? This was Nicole's house. He was Nicole's former stepson. In a strange way that sort of made him responsible in Nicole's absence. Not that he *wanted* to be responsible but…?

Decision made. Seb swung his legs down from the recliner and nodded. 'I can see that could be a problem. How about you show me how Milou made his escape? Then maybe between the two of us we can come up with a plan to keep him safe from now on. What do you say?'

The little boy glanced back towards Ella and Milou, twisted his mouth from side to side, made a decision, and said, 'My name is Daniel. What's yours?'

'Well, back in Australia my friends call me Seb. How about that?'

'Okay,' Dan replied with a shrug as he meshed his little fingers into Seb's open hand and tried to drag him off towards the barn.

Seb stood in silence and glanced down at Dan's small fingers clasped tightly around his. He hadn't been expecting that. Some of his team were married with children but the majority of the technical experts who worked with him in design were single men. He was not used to having children around him in his workplace or his daily life.

Especially children who insisted on holding his hand. He could not recall that ever happening before.

This was going to be a first. But he was up for new experiences. He could handle it.

'Come on, Seb,' Dan called out, and tugged at his hand. 'Or Wolfie will break Milou out again.'

Ella watched as Seb paused for a second, dumbfounded, before closing his fingers around her son's relatively tiny fist and walking slowly back out to the sunlit garden. Dan's little dark head kept glancing up as he chatted nonstop about the fence and the gaps between the trees, and how his mum and Yvette had fixed them high on one side, but Wolfie had jumped on the fence when he came to see Milou and it all just went squish, and…

Seb nodded but did not reply. He had opened up a personal organiser one-handed and was probably looking for the telephone number of a local odd-jobs man at that very minute. This of course was what *she* should have done. If she had thought of it.

How could he get a word in? Dan had said more than enough for both of them.

Oh, Dan.

Ella hadn't been expecting that outburst about his dad. Dan was wonderful with adults he knew, but he sometimes found it difficult to approach men. Especially strangers he had never met before.

She sat and watched the unlikely pair for a few seconds in silence. The tall business executive in the designer clothing, wearing shoes that cost more than her week's wages, was giving his full attention to a little boy who was revelling in the simple fact that he had a man to talk to for once.

A man who did not have other children to deal with and play with.

A man Dan could talk to and keep all to himself. Even it was only for a short while.

And her heart broke for her fatherless child who would never know the love his father had felt for him. One day she might find someone who loved both her and Dan, but in the meantime she could only hope that Dan did not become too attached to Seb in the short time that he was going to be with them.

Perhaps having Seb in the house for a few days was not such a good idea after all?

CHAPTER FOUR

SEB turned over in bed, pulled an overstuffed pillow over his head and decided that there was no way he could go back to sleep.

His body clock was still set on Sydney time, and it was too dark and quiet in his old room for his brain to calm itself long enough for sleep. His mind was still racing with the exhilaration of the events of the last two days and he had tossed and turned most of the night. Twice he had reached out to the bedside table and typed a couple of notes on his personal organiser.

He was totally exhilarated at the prospect of completing the deal with PSN Media—but more than a little frustrated that he had come all the way out here to see Nicole only to find her still on holiday. Both of which had conspired to rob him of sleep.

Seb tossed aside his pillow.

Back in Sydney Nicole was famous for being the least sporty person he had known, which was quite an achievement in *that* city. And now she was trekking in Nepal? She certainly had changed in the last three years—it would have been nice to catch up. But unless Nicole managed to get back to France in the next thirty-six hours, he was going to leave without seeing her. And he was sorry for that.

But now it was time to make a move.

Untangling himself out of the mess of twisted bedcovers, Seb tested the temperature of the cool floor tiles on his bare feet and shuffled across the room in his T-shirt and shorts to open the window. It would not take him long to repack his hand luggage.

It had made sense for him to stay here overnight but he could work a lot more effectively back in Montpellier with Matt and a hard wire connection to the Internet rather than a wireless telephone connection.

Warm sunlight slanted in, startlingly bright and welcoming, then blinding him with the brilliance of a summer sunrise as he pushed open the shutters.

In an instant his old boyhood bedroom was transformed in that unique quality of light in the Languedoc that reflected back from the tall ivory-painted walls.

The honey-coloured armoire, which had seemed so bizarre and antiquated the previous evening, now looked perfect set against the pastel colour scheme that had been chosen for the textiles in the room.

He ran his forefinger along the faded floral stencils of leaves and pale pink flowers and wondered what gentle hand had worked the design with such care and detail.

One thing was for sure.

This furniture and this decor had certainly not been here eighteen years ago. Back then this house had been clean, comfortable, and a home. Now he felt as though he had just spent the night in some theatre set for a typical French country house.

All the pictures were perfectly parallel to the floor and every square centimetre of exposed wood had been sanded and waxed to create one uniform sheen. Imperfections were clearly not allowed.

But it *was* beautiful. Stylish and what you would expect to find in this part of France.

For a hotel room.

Pushing harder on the shutters, he leant forward onto the stone window sill and looked out across the garden at the back of the house. Some things had not changed.

And his senses reeled at the sensory overload.

The early morning sun shimmered hot above the terracotta roof tiles, distorting the cobalt blue of the sky with ripples and waves of colour. Any cloud had already been burnt away to leave a pristine expanse of unbroken clear sky.

He breathed in the air, fragrant and clean. Somewhere in the distance dogs were barking and he could just about detect the rumble of traffic on the nearby road he had driven down the previous evening, but apart from that there was only birdsong.

And the sound of a woman's voice singing somewhere in the garden below.

It was such a sweet sound that at first he thought it must be a radio station or recording, but as he listened the song was broken up by snatches of humming and a gentle sniff followed by a strange sequence of made-up words and tunes.

The sound was so intriguing, bizarre and interesting that he could not help but smile just hearing it. It was somehow—joyous. As though the owner wanted to express out loud her love of life and living and music.

And that spirit and energy was so contagious there should be a health warning!

The vague headache that had been nagging him for days seemed to lift away as he listened and he could feel his shoulders unclench.

Suddenly he didn't want to stand inside and look *out* at the warmth and the sunshine. He wanted to experience it for himself. He wanted to immerse himself in this place he used to know so well for a few more moments before he headed back to the city and the luxury of a five-star hotel conference room.

Getting dressed could wait. His normal urge to turn on his laptop and log onto his international Wi-Fi connection. Could wait. *Well, for now anyway. He would be back on the road in an hour.*

It took only a few minutes for Seb to skip down the stone stairs, draw open the wide front door and stroll out barefoot onto the golden sandstone paving that curved around the side wall of the house to the part of the patio that was bathed in sunlight.

Seb's brain tried to assimilate the intensity of the colours he was looking at. And failed.

Lavender bushes lined the paths and exploded in long swathes in huge clipped hedges, mixed with what looked like pale blue bellflowers and pink peonies in full bloom. Rambling roses covered the stone wall above glossy dark green leaves.

Dominating the garden was the old pollarded plane tree that had been planted when the house was built. Large flat leaves provided perfect dappled shade over the patio area outside the kitchen door all summer.

Birdsong filled the air. Mixed with the lapping of water on stones from the nearby river. Otherwise there was only the hum of bees on the flowers.

It was so quiet it felt as though he were the only human being for miles.

Perhaps he had imagined that musical voice and was still half dreaming after all?

The warm breeze was fragrant with the scent of flowers and herbs. And something else—a scent that was unique to this special garden. Rich and sweet and spicy. Like cinnamon apples, only sweeter.

One sniff of that scent and he was taken back to his life in this house. Dozens of white rose blossoms cascaded out of the urns and trailed in profusion up into a white-painted trellis on the wall of the house where the rose branches were intertwined with sweet white jasmine to create a heady aroma.

Musk rose and jasmine. It was wonderful. Magical. His mother would have loved it.

A bristle of discomfort shivered across his back.

Helene Castellano was the only mother that he had ever known. The fact that she might not be his birth mother did not change the close bond that they had shared. He was so proud of her and everything she represented.

Except that, as he looked around this garden, the thoughts and concerns he had pushed to the back of his mind since he had found out that his dad was not his father started to slip through gaps in the barriers he had put in place. Each fresh memory of his life in this house rose like a bubble to the surface, bringing with it fresh concerns.

Seb sucked in a deep breath of the fragrant warm air.

Despite his best intentions, he was still infuriated with his dad for refusing to discuss the matter of his parentage with him. And he simply did not understand why he did not want to tell him the truth. It was illogical. They were adults and it had all happened thirty years ago.

He could at the very least have told him whether he had another father, or whether he had been adopted! He would not have judged his mother any differently if she had a previous relationship before marrying Luc Castellano six months before he was born. Everyone made mistakes in life. And she had been a wonderful mother to him.

What if he had been adopted? Perhaps there was a family out there looking for him? He did not need one, but it was something to consider.

Unless of course there was something about his real parents that his dad did not want him to know. Something that could be damaging to him, and possibly even his career? That was possible—but if anything it made his need to find out the truth even more pressing.

Perhaps their hasty emigration to Australia had been because of his real father?

He had so many questions and so few answers.

Seb closed his eyes and fought to calm his racing mind.

This was not what he was here for. That was in the past. *He would persuade his dad to tell him when he got back to Sydney.* Perhaps he could take some photos of the place before he left? Just to remind his dad of their happy family life in this house? It could be just the extra ammunition he needed to help change his mind.

This was probably why Seb stepped out from under the shade of the patio onto the hot stone and pressed his bare toes onto the warmth beneath his feet.

The heat seemed to radiate upwards like energy from the earth until it reached his head and he leant backwards to take in the maximum amount of the glorious warmth on his head and throat.

The balmy breeze caressed his face, shoulders and exposed lower arms.

With one breath he closed his eyes and wallowed in the moment.

Serene. Tranquil. Warm. Heaven. He could stay like this for ever. Arms outstretched.

He was instantly transported back to another time in this very garden and his life as a boy. Memories flooded into his head. Memories he had not even thought about for many years, memories buried deep down inside his private life, which the paparazzi would never know about or expose to the public world.

Memories of gentle hands and kind adult voices saying how sorry they were, and how much they would miss her. His grandmother in black. Friends and neighbours, school pals.

His mother had died in her favourite month of the year. And that was more than sad. She would have enjoyed this garden.

His reverie was broken by a snuffling noise coming from the direction of the kitchen to his right, followed by the unmistakeable sound of the same woman's voice, humming along to an old show tune.

Seb slowly opened his eyes, dropped his arms in alarm like a teenager caught with his hands in the cookie jar, and whipped around to check that nobody had seen him so exposed. His neck flared red with embarrassment at the thought that Ella Martinez and her son were probably both awake and sniggering at him through the bedroom curtains!

He had already embarrassed himself enough talking to Dan about his dad without adding to the humiliation.

Of course there had been no way of knowing that Dan's father had passed away, but it was still an awkward moment and he felt for the boy and his mother. He knew what it was like to lose a parent and Dan was so young. That was tough.

As it was he had barely spent more than an hour with Ella and Dan the previous evening before excusing himself to a couple of intense hours spent in the company of his laptop, a two-day backlog of emails and a delicious meal Ella had delivered to his room on a tray.

This probably explained his grumbling stomach in need of breakfast.

Time to find the source of the singing! And something quick to eat so that he could get packed and back to civilisation—and away from these unsettling memories.

By following the sweet voice Seb strolled slowly around the patio, his bare feet finding an occasional piece of loose gravel, but it was worth it.

Ella Martinez was standing just inside the kitchen door,

whisking something in a large ceramic bowl. She was dancing and jiggling her head from side to side. A telltale pair of white headset wires trailed down to the pocket of her pink pyjamas.

Her right arm was beating in tune with the song she was humming, which sounded as if it should be from a classical musical, but he could not place it.

Her hips and shoulders twisted and turned and as he watched she lifted a wooden spoon and conducted a virtual orchestra on the other side of the kitchen window, so caught up in her world that he felt guilty at the very thought of intruding.

The sunlight was on one side of Ella's face, flashing the copper and gold highlights in her long brown hair that fell about her shoulders. She looked rapturous and as innocent as the day.

It was a moment and a view he knew would stay with him. No photograph could have captured it. The smell of the flowers early in the morning, the tang of the pine trees, the sound of songbirds in the trees.

And a pretty brunette dancing in a country kitchen.

It was all combined into one magical moment in time.

A familiar heat welled inside him, and despite his best intentions Seb wondered how a grown woman old enough to have a little boy like Dan could look so sexy and desirable in pyjamas with pink rabbits on them.

She was so totally different from the kind of woman he normally was attracted to, but somehow, in this house and this garden, she was perfect.

He envied her total sense of relaxed serenity and the calm lifestyle that came from living in a country farmhouse. Her day might be spent within the small world of this house and garden but he could think of worse places to live.

It was not Sydney. It couldn't be. His apartment was within

walking distance of world-class restaurants and entertainment. But calm? No.

One more reason for him to get back to his own world as soon as he could. No doubt about it. This place was seriously unsettling, even if he did enjoy the view.

Ella was humming as she moved between a long pine kitchen table and the granite worktop of a very modern-looking professional-standard kitchen.

Ella Martinez was not just pretty. She was unspoilt, unsophisticated and completely charming. And disarming. Part of him wanted to know more about the woman behind the façade of mother and housekeeper.

Which unsettled him even more.

Perhaps it was this house that was the cause of such thinking?

And yet…the attraction was there.

He should ask her if she had heard anything from Nicole. Keep it formal and fast.

Then he remembered that he was in boxers and a T-shirt. Unshaven and in need of a shower. Perhaps not his best look. Time to make a discreet retreat back to his room to get changed.

Too late. Just as he turned Milou snuffled his way across the patio from the direction of the barn and the woods, saw him, stopped dead, ears up, then hurled itself in Seb's direction, tail wagging. And started barking furiously.

Seb groaned and the dog jumped up onto his scanty clothing trying to make purchase on thin cloth not designed for dog claws but this time he managed to stay on his feet by sitting on the edge of the patio table. Oh, no, not again. And ouch.

Instantly he heard a low whistle and looked up as Ella strolled out of the kitchen, her wooden spatula dripping in one hand. Milou leapt towards his food bowl, leaving Seb to try and salvage his dignity and modesty with a bright, 'Good morning, Mrs Martinez.'

Exposed.

Ella wondered how long he had been watching her.

A flush of the heat of embarrassment flared at Ella's neck under the hairline and she shook it off. It was done now.

And it might have been worse. Some days she only wore the T-shirt! Nicole usually brought a female friend to stay or a gentleman guest who made himself scarce in the most discreet way.

And Sebastien Castellano was going to be here for a few days!

With a bit of luck his early-morning wander around the garden was the exception rather than the rule.

She loved her music and this short time before Dan woke was so precious, she claimed it for herself. For an hour or so each morning she could indulge in her passion for her music without waking Dan by playing the piano in the salon or singing too loudly.

Ella swallowed down her embarrassment, lifted her chin and smiled politely as though she were greeting a garden-party guest and waved at him as graciously as she could with her wooden spoon, especially considering that they were both in their nightwear.

'Good morning to you. And it's Ella, remember?' she replied. 'I hope that you slept well. It's a lovely morning.'

The smell of warm earth, the garden flowers and a salty citrus tang of man sweat and whatever body spray he used hit her hard, then hit her again as she moved closer to shake his hand. Except one of her hands was holding a mixing bowl and the other was sticky with splashes of batter from the wooden spoon.

His dark eyes under darker eyebrows flickered with

something close to amusement as she changed her mind and simply gestured with her spoon instead.

Even in shorts that revealed long powerful legs and a taut waist, Sebastien was every inch the sophisticated city millionaire businessman. And he was tall. At least a foot taller than she was. But there was also a presence about Seb. A gravitas that screamed loud and clear that this was a man who was used to giving orders and seeing them through.

The main effect it had on her was to make her gabble to fill the silence between them.

'And if you don't like Ella some of my friends call me Cindy. You know—Cinderella. Like the fairy story. But I'll answer to either Ella or Cindy. You choose.'

She looked into his slightly stunned face and wondered if her Beatrix Potter T-shirt and pink pyjama bottoms were too much for that time in the morning. And she wasn't wearing anything underneath.

And she had messy unbrushed bed hair.

Oh, no. Not exactly the best look. The village was used to her creative dress sense. From the look on her employer's stepson's face, Seb was clearly not.

'Ella,' he said, sounding out the letters, 'is perfect. But only if you call me Seb.'

She opened her mouth to suggest Bastien or Sebby or Bast, and changed her mind. If this man wanted to be called Seb she could live with it.

Seb was staring into her face so intently that she wondered if the pancake batter had splashed on her cheek or there was a pillow feather sticking out of her hair.

'Thank you. Seb. Was the room okay? I am sorry if I woke you with my crazy singing this morning. I'll try and remember to be quiet in the future.'

'The room was fine. And you are free to sing any time

you like. This is Nicole's house and your home. Speaking of which, have you heard from Nicole?'

Ella felt the tension in the air lift to match the sudden stiffness in his shoulders. And his dark eyebrows grew even more hooded.

'Not yet, but I haven't fired up my computer yet this morning. I'm just about to get dressed then make some breakfast, Seb. Would you like to join us in, say, twenty minutes and I can check my mail? Then I need to bring you up to date about the birthday party.'

She paused and sucked in a breath. 'Things are going to be a little *interesting* around here today.'

The first thing Seb heard when he walked down the corridor to the kitchen was a series of big sighs followed by groans. Perhaps that was what Ella had meant by 'interesting'.

The shower had been hot. His suit trousers and business shirt were relatively uncreased and as he tied the laces in his shiny black shoes his uniform was complete and his brain more or less back to the state he was used to.

In control and focused on the task in hand.

His ten minutes of madness in the sun were over. He had things to do and people to see and a full agenda of work to get through—depending on when Nicole was expected back from holiday.

Perhaps Nicole could meet them at the airport?

What was really annoying him was that he didn't have the information he needed at his fingertips. Yes, of course Nicole would make contact with her housekeeper as first point of call, but he found it surprisingly frustrating to be kept out of the loop.

He checked his watch. Twenty minutes. Precisely. Ella should have logged on by now and picked up any emails.

So he was not quite prepared for the sight of Dan sitting

at the kitchen table with his chin in his hands, his face only inches from the screen of the oldest TV Seb had ever seen in his life.

'Mu-u-um, it doesn't work, Mum. I can't see Aunty Nicole *at all*!'

'I'll be right there, sweetheart. Just enjoy your breakfast.'

Ella had changed from kids' pyjamas into slim-fitting cherry-coloured trousers and a sleeveless candy-stripe top in pinks and yellows. It was a riot of colour and he felt oddly drab and sombre. Perhaps he should have packed some casual clothing? He only ever carried hand luggage on business flights, which did not leave any room for casual clothing, but he just might be a tad too formally dressed for a French farmhouse.

It was only as he moved closer that Seb realised that the TV was connected to a huge computer case with a well-worn keyboard and mouse attached.

This wasn't a TV. It was a personal computer. And, from the age of it, was probably powered by a steam engine.

Another long sigh came from Dan and the little boy's shoulders dropped even lower as Ella placed a brightly coloured plate with delicious-looking billowy fruit pancakes and a glass of milk in front of him.

'Hello, Dan.' Seb smiled down at the face that was twisted into a curious expression as Dan chewed. 'What have you got there?'

Dan gulped down his bit of pancake and waved the remaining portion towards the monitor, scattering soft crumbs onto the keyboard and table as he did so.

'Aunty Nicole sent a letter and pictures of elephants! And big mountains with snow.'

'And where exactly are these mountains, Dan?' Ella asked.

His lips twisted for a second and then he nodded with a big grin. 'India. The elephants are in India.'

Ella glanced once at Seb, then shrugged. 'Close enough. Well done for remembering.' She gestured to the table. 'Please join us, Seb—I will have some scrambled eggs and ham ready in two minutes.'

'Wonderful,' he replied, his stomach growling in agreement, but as he looked at the display of large-size pancakes, croissants, preserves and baguette laid out for a more adult breakfast at the end of the long table furthest away from Dan Seb made his second executive decision of the day and sat down in the chair next to the little boy and leant forward so that they could stare at the screen together.

The Internet browser did have emails, but the photographs attached to the message were taking so long to open up that Dan would be in school before he saw anything.

'Um, see what you mean. Mind if I have a go?'

'Mum. Is it okay if Seb touches the 'puter?'

Seb glanced up at Ella, who was still stirring eggs, and she smiled at him and nodded. 'Only if he promises not to break it,' she replied with a smirk, her teeth pressed into her lower lip to block the laughter.

'Oh, I promise,' Seb replied earnestly, and Dan looked at him, nodded once and passed him the mouse so that he could concentrate on holding his beaker of milk with both hands.

It had been a very long time since Seb had seen such a decrepit piece of equipment with the processing speed of a small slug. In fact his mobile phone had better connections.

Just as Ella was bringing the pan of eggs towards the table, Seb pushed back his chair. 'Back in a moment, please start without me.'

In fact it took him a good few minutes to jog up to his room, slip back to the kitchen with his laptop and forward the email to himself so that Dan could read the message on the laptop instead of the TV screen.

'Here you are, Dan.'

'Where's the clicky mouse?'

'Inside. You press on here instead. And that little box sticking out of the side means that I can connect to the Internet wherever I go in the world.'

Dan's eyes widened in delight. And he yelled out loud and clapped his hands together as a brightly coloured photo of a woman smiled back at him with a dramatic backdrop of ice and mountains.

'Look, Mum—it's Aunty Nicole.'

Ella took a second to spoon the creamy scrambled eggs onto ham and toasted sourdough bread on Seb's breakfast plate, then lifted the hot pan away from Dan's head and peered over his shoulder.

'It certainly is. Look at that lovely hat she is wearing! Thank you, Seb. That was very thoughtful. Please. Feel free to read the message. It's not private.'

Dan nodded several times as he chewed and mumbled his thanks through a full mouth.

Seb smiled back. 'You are most welcome.' And then his smile faded. 'She's not due back in Paris until Monday evening, and then plans to fly south late Tuesday.'

He sat back and pursed his lips. 'Well, that's a shame. I was hoping to see Nicole but I have to fly home late Monday.'

Seb glanced up at Ella. 'My apologies, Mrs Martinez, but in that case there is no reason to stay here any longer. I'll drive back to Montpellier later this morning.'

Dan's eyes widened in astonishment. 'You have to leave? Already?'

Ella kissed the top of Dan's head, her hands on his shoulders, but the smile had faded from her mouth. 'Don't you remember what Aunty Nicole said? This is Seb's work. He lives in Australia and that is a long way from here. Now. Time to check on Milou and get ready for school. Okay?'

Dan nodded furiously while sliding off his chair, a pancake clutched in one hand, but stopped to pat Seb on the arm.

'Can I send you a mailey message on the 'puter? Please? Can I?'

'Sure,' Seb replied, between mouthfuls, and then shot a glance towards Ella. 'If it's okay with your mum.'

Ella looked from Seb to Dan, then grinned. 'Maybe later.'

Ella sat down opposite Seb as soon as Dan had skipped up the staircase and exhaled loudly before she poured two cups of fragrant coffee.

'I am so sorry about that,' she said in a low voice. 'Dan seems to love anything to do with computers and technology. I have no idea where he gets that from.'

Then she looked up at him with a faint smile. 'I am sorry that you have to leave so soon. I know Nicole will be very disappointed to have missed you. She was so looking forward to having you here.'

Seb took a long sip of the delicious coffee, and savoured the aroma and flavour with a satisfied sigh.

'As am I, but I do have a question. You are clearly an excellent cook, Ella, but you are also a busy mum. I'm surprised that Nicole asked you to organise her birthday party. That's a lot of work for one person.'

Seb reached into a pocket and pulled out his personal organiser. 'If it helps, I could make amends for my absence by arranging for an events management company to take care of the party. I would be happy to do it.'

Ella replied with several quick shakes of the head.

'Thank you, but no, Seb. Nicole didn't ask me to organise her birthday. I volunteered. I asked *her* to give me the chance to do it.'

* * *

Just as Ella was about to tell him the long list of reasons there was a sharp knock on the kitchen door and a small dark-haired older woman with bow knees sauntered in, nodded at Seb, deposited a basket of what looked like apricots on the kitchen floor, then kissed Ella on each cheek before heading back to the breakfast table.

Ella's friend was wearing blue dungarees and old boots set off with a jaunty wool scarf. She leant against the sink and slurped down the coffee as Ella dived into the box.

'Oh, these are fantastic!' Ella squealed in perfect French with enough of the local accent that Seb could not help but be impressed. Unless you had been born and raised in this area, most people did not notice the subtle differences between the dialects in the different towns of the Languedoc. But Ella seemed to have picked it up perfectly.

Then she looked up and remembered that Seb had no clue as to who their visitor was.

'Oh, sorry. Introductions. Yvette. Do you remember the Castellano family who used to live here? This is Sebastien Castellano visiting from Sydney.'

'Of course I remember,' Yvette replied and nodded once. 'You're Helene's son. Used to play football with my boys after school when we had the farm.' She scanned his business clothing for a few seconds before adding, 'I heard that you've done well for yourself.' Then she slurped down what was left of the coffee, grabbed another pancake and waved one hand in the air with a friendly goodbye and was gone before Seb had a chance to reply.

'What was that all about?' Seb asked in a dazed voice.

'Actually that was quite a speech for Yvette,' Ella replied. 'The forecast is for a mistral storm over the weekend and I need to bring in the cherries today or risk losing them.'

She stopped rummaging around inside the basket and glanced back towards the kitchen door before whispering in

English, 'Yvette is a wonderful babysitter and totally brilliant with the garden, but I am a bit worried that she'll try to help me out from the top of a wobbly ladder in the orchard, so, would you mind doing me a huge favour?'

Ella licked her lips a couple of times. 'Could you keep Yvette talking and away from ladders until I get back from the school run? I don't want any accidents, but I promise that I won't be long and you can get on your way the minute I get back.'

Then she gave him a lopsided grin. 'I was forgetting! This is your chance to catch up with all of the gossip. Won't that be the best fun?'

CHAPTER FIVE

BEING interrogated by Yvette for almost an hour about every detail of where he had been, what he had studied, what he had done and where he had travelled in the past eighteen years had not been what Seb called fun.

And she had made him work. By the time Ella wheeled her bicycle around the corner of the house, he had emptied three wheelbarrows of plant clippings, heard potted histories of most of his old schoolmates and made rash promises to welcome assorted members of Yvette's extended family to Sydney.

So he was more than happy to hand over the reins to Ella, who vanished into the kitchen with Yvette the minute she got back, leaving him trapped outside on the patio.

At last! It was finally time to get packed and on his way back to the business world he understood.

So he had to find a way into the house that did not involve going through the kitchen. The fastest way would be to sneak in through the sitting room and what had been his mother's *salon*.

Sebastien glanced through the open patio windows of the long wide room and stopped dead in his tracks—his feet frozen to the floor.

Hanging above the heavy stone mantelpiece of the original

fireplace was a photograph he had never seen in his life. Of his mother.

Tears pricked at the corners of his eyes, startling him with their intensity, after the shock of seeing her picture, life size, smiling back at him.

Hardly believing his eyes, he clenched his toes hard inside his made-to-measure shoes and breathed out slowly through his nose before taking a step across the threshold onto the marble tiles.

Only the fireplace was familiar in this strange mix of a room that had originally been two rooms—the formal parlour and the *salon*. The dividing wall was gone and the long sitting-room windows had been replaced by wide glass doors that opened out into the garden and allowed light to flood into what had been a rather dark space.

That light seemed focused like a spotlight on his mother's image. She must have been in her twenties when the photograph was taken and the photographer had captured her in a moment when every aspect of her beauty and grace were at their height.

She looked stunning. More like a film actress or professional fashion model than the woman who had kissed him goodnight and made his favourite chocolate cake every Friday—just because she felt like it.

How had he forgotten how very beautiful she had been?

Her sparkling hazel-green and amber eyes shone out from the flat surface behind the glass, as bright as her perfect smile that could light up any room in seconds. Even now this simple colour photograph dominated the room.

She was wearing a pale pink dress with the slight shimmer of silk in the ruffles on the collar, and a single string of pearls he knew that his father still kept in a wooden box in his bedroom that Seb was not supposed to know about.

On one shoulder was a corsage of white and pale pink

rosebuds chosen to match the exact same shade as her dress and she had raised her left hand towards it. She was wearing a ring with a large heart-shaped diamond-cut pink stone on the fourth finger—but it was not a ring he recognised.

Intrigued and fascinated by the maelstrom of emotions whirling around inside him, Seb moved closer to the fireplace until he was within touching distance of what was obviously an amateur photograph.

One thing was clear. She was looking straight into the lens of the camera and at the person taking the photograph with a look in her eyes that was absolutely unmistakable. It was the look of love. Because if Helene Castellano had a flaw, this was it.

She was incapable of hiding her true feelings—about anything.

She might have told him that the garden frog he had presented her with when he was seven was the best she had ever seen, but he had only had to look at her face to know the truth. And she had released the poor frog back into the river by morning.

He had loved her so very much. When she was taken ill, he had felt so powerless to do anything to help her that her last weeks were a whirlwind of kind words and fierce anger and frustration, which he took out on everyone and everything around him.

In life she had taught him about respect and hard work. Her death had taught him what it felt like to love someone so much and then have that love snatched away from you.

Her heart had been an open book.

His heart was locked tight closed and was going to stay that way. Other men might be foolish enough to risk falling in love and start a family. Not for him.

The blood pounded in the veins in his neck.

The photograph could have been taken by Luc Castellano,

the man he had called his father for the first thirty years of his life. But it could equally have been a friend or relative at the same party. He simply could not know! And yet this photograph had been deliberately left behind when they emigrated!

Possibilities raced through his mind in tune with the blood pounding in his heart. What if his birth parents had been in the same room when this photograph was taken?

This photograph could be the clue he had not even acknowledged that he had been looking for. The first step to finding the answers to so many questions he had buried deep inside about his parentage.

Questions which now *burned* to be answered.

He had been a fool.

The growing feeling of unease and anxiety that had sat on his shoulders ever since he found out that his dad could not be his natural father suddenly made sense.

It had nothing to do with the business deal, and everything to do with understanding who he truly was, and the decisions his parents had taken to give him a safe family life.

Instead of feeling elation and exhilaration that he was within sight of the greatest business deal of his life, standing at that moment in front of his mother's portrait, all he could feel was a hollow emptiness that needed to be filled.

The Helene Castellano Foundation meant everything to him going forward and he refused to let that work suffer because he was preoccupied with his heritage and his past. He *had* to put that behind him.

He had come here to ease his mind before starting work on the greatest adventure of his life. Nicole was not around. So he would have to do the job himself.

It was time to face the facts and get the answers he needed.

* * *

There was a rustle of movement behind Seb and he swung around, his mouth hard with emotion and resentful at the intrusion.

Ella bustled happily through the patio doors, her arms wrapped around a china bowl packed with a stunning arrangement of fresh early sunflowers and green foliage, which she carefully lowered onto the low coffee table in front of the sofas, turning the bowl from side to side to give the best viewpoint.

Only when she was satisfied did she stand back, nod once, and then march over to the *dressoir* sideboard and start rummaging around in a long bottom drawer.

'Thank you for staying and looking after Yvette. Do you like the portrait? I found your mum's photograph in a box in the attic. Nicole's designer had some modern abstract above the fireplace but it was totally wrong. Doesn't she look wonderful?'

Her words had emerged with such a gush and a rush that Seb had to take a second to form an answer.

'Yes, she does,' he replied, turning back to face the portrait so that Ella could not see his face as he composed himself. 'I've never actually seen that picture before. I don't have many family photographs so it's quite a surprise.'

Ella shoved the drawer closed and pushed herself back onto her feet with a satisfied sigh. 'Here is the original print. These were all in the same box in the attic.'

Seb stared at the brown card wallet that Ella was holding out towards him and steadied himself to accept it from her, only they both stepped forwards at the same time and for a fraction of a second their fingers slid into contact, a gentle stroke of skin against sensitive skin.

Instantly a burst of hot energy ran through Seb's hand, then arm and body, like a small electric shock. It was so unexpected and surprising that he half coughed out loud, breaking the heavy weight of silence. The awkwardness of the moment made him look up from the folder into Ella's blue, blue eyes. And found that she was staring back at him. Wide eyed. Startled.

In a blink she sucked in a breath, waved her arms to the air above her head and squeaked. 'More in the attic. I'll go and, er, try and find them for you.'

Before Seb could reply Ella fled away into the corridor, her sandals making a light pattering on the wooden staircase.

Clearly he had not been the only one to feel the connection.

Mentally shaking himself for being so obvious in front of a widowed single mother, Seb sighed heavily.

More photographs? He didn't even know that these photographs existed, and here they were. For *strangers* to see.

He flicked open the folder, and quickly sorted through the jumble of mostly black and white prints he found inside.

Some of the faces were so familiar to him they were like friends he vaguely remembered but could not name. His grandmother and his parents were in many of them, but in others strangers smiled back from locations and events from a very different world he knew nothing about—a world called the past.

Then he found it. A small colour print with his mother smiling out. Her beauty and life force captured in two dimensions for all time. Only as he picked it up he saw that there was writing on the back.

His heart skipped a beat as he read the faded words in French. *'Engagement Party. 26 May. André's house.'*

That was all. No indication of who had been celebrating their engagement. Or who André was. A friend? A relative?

Perhaps André was one of the young people in the bundle of photographs he had just glanced at? Someone who had known his mother as a young woman and who could tell him who his birth parents had been and what had happened to them.

He had so many questions. And way, way, too few answers.

Seb dropped the folder of photographs onto the sofa and started pacing up and down the room between the fireplace and the garden.

He had known the old house would have mixed memories for him, but this was something new. Something he could not have expected.

Hot resentment flashed through him and his fingers clenched into his palms. His dad had left these precious photographs of his mother and his heritage behind in his rush to abandon everything and leave for a tiny apartment in Sydney.

Seb stopped pacing and picked up the colour print. How could he do it? How could he have left these pictures behind for strangers like Ella Martinez to sort through? Maybe even throw out or burn in the fire? He could easily have made room for these few precious pieces of paper.

Back in Sydney he had three photographs of his mother. Three worn, faded and torn prints, the surface coating worn away by the rubbing of his fingers over the years. His dad had one single wedding photo in a silver frame in his bedroom, which Seb used to sneak in and look at. He never got tired of grinning back at the pretty dark-haired girl in a long white dress and carrying a huge bouquet of flowers that trailed almost to the ground, standing next to his dad in his best banker's smart suit, as they both smiled for the camera.

Four photographs. And yet here in this house he had already seen more photographs than he ever knew existed.

It was almost as if his dad had deliberately kept these photos from him. Was he trying to hide something? Trying to protect him?

Not any more.

Change of plan.

He was here now. He had the means and the opportunity and he could spare a few hours of personal time. In a few days he would be back to Australia. This could be the only chance he might have.

The more he thought about it, the more decisive he became.

He had used his tenacity and determination to take his business to the top. Now it was time to apply that same energy and drive to do some digging into his own past.

Decision made.

He had a new mission. *He was going to find any and every scrap of evidence of his family's past.* Even if it meant turning this house upside down to find them.

Starting with the attic.

Because whatever he found from now on, he had every intention of claiming for himself. This was personal and had nothing whatsoever to do with Nicole or her housekeeper. Nothing at all.

Ella tried to wind her way through the jumble of unwanted furniture and assorted objects that had accumulated in the attic. And fought a sudden urge to kick them out of the way. Hard.

Stamping her foot, she squeezed her eyes tight shut, dropped her head back and counted to ten. Backwards. The furniture was bashed enough without her adding to the knocks and scrapes.

They said that bad things came in threes. Well, her Friday was certainly turning out to be a lot more challenging than she had expected. First was the news about the mistral. A summer storm was the last thing this garden needed a few days before a garden party. And it could last for days!

As for the second? It was obvious to her now that Sebastien

Castellano never had any intention of staying around long enough to attend Nicole's birthday party. And that was just cruel.

How could he do that? How could he promise to be here then change his mind?

She simply did not understand that at all. He had travelled halfway around the world for a business trip, only to take off again without seeing Nicole!

How could he be so selfish? Surely he could put Nicole's needs in front of his own for once? And what was so urgent back in Sydney that he could not stay for a few more days?

And then there was the killer. The thick letter stuffed into her trouser pocket that had been waiting for her when she got back from the school run.

The very sight of the Spanish stamps made her heart sink into her deck shoes.

To a six-year-old, Barcelona might just as well have been next to India and not just a few hours' drive away. Not that Christobal's parents came to see them very often. They hated staying at Sandrine's clean but simple hotel and made repeated comparisons with their luxury villa complete with indoor heated swimming pool and every possible item of the latest technology.

They truly could not tolerate the fact that their grandson was being brought up in a tiny French village while their daughter-in-law worked as a housekeeper for a wealthy woman.

She did not even drive any more.

Christmas had been a nightmare. As soon as Dan had gone to bed they had bombarded her with their elaborate plans for his education—all the time making her feel like a completely selfish mother by not providing personal tutors and modern computer games and the like so that Dan would not feel left out at the expensive private schools he would soon be attending.

Yeah. Boarding schools. Right. Like she was going to let that happen! Except of course by selfishly keeping Dan here with her she was ruining his chance of a good education and a career. Guilt. Guilt. Guilt.

Ella groaned, then shrugged and sat down on the curved cover of an old trunk and opened the letter under the light beaming in through the dirty glass-covered skylight in the attic roof.

Then hot tears burned the corners of her eyes, blurring her vision.

Two return train tickets to Barcelona. First class. For Monday next week! Two days. She only had two days before she had to hand her baby boy over to his grandparents.

Oh, no. Of course she had known that they wanted to see Dan during his summer school holidays, but the first week! The Martinez family took their holiday in August, not July! And Dan had been so looking forward to Nicole's party. If she used these tickets, she would be forced to leave him there on his own while she scurried back here to work every hour she could to create this very special birthday party for Nicole.

So what if she had been putting on a brave face in front of Sebastien Castellano? He didn't have to know that she was secretly panicking. Swan on the water did not come close.

No. She would simply reschedule the dates and… Ella scan-read the letter that came with the tickets. His grandparents had already booked more tickets for a whole programme of special trips and wonderful treats for Dan, which she knew that he would adore.

The energy and the fight drained out of her.

She couldn't reschedule the trip without throwing all of those plans away.

They were Christobal's parents! Of course they wanted to

see Dan and give him a wonderful time. Dan was all they had left of their son. Chris would have wanted this. Of course, Chris would also have liked them to welcome her as well. But that was a lot more difficult.

Her fingers clenched around the paper. What choice did she have? They knew that she did not have the money to give Dan the things they could. Playing the piano at Sandrine's at the weekends was not going to be enough to even buy a new computer. She was lucky to have Sandrine's old machine so that she could keep in touch with her own parents and they were in no position to help her financially.

In their eyes she had made a total mess of her life. A wandering musician without a stable home. She had no investments or resources to provide her son with the type of education that his father had enjoyed. She had never even been to university!

The beam of sunshine focused through the skylight on her hand and she watched tiny motes of dust float in and out of the narrow cone of intense light. Dust particles going where the breeze took them. Without direction.

Then the sound of a dog barking echoed up from the garden and the old house creaked around her. Solid and reassuring.

'Stupid girl,' she said out loud, wiped her eyes with a not-so-clean finger and sniffed loudly. She was *not* without direction or friends. 'Let's get this show on the road. Things to do and people to see.'

'Do you have a saying for everything, Mrs Martinez?' a man's voice asked, and Ella practically jumped off the trunk in shock.

Seb watched Ella stuff a letter into her trouser pocket. He had seen enough for him to know that something had upset her very badly.

'I'm sorry if I startled you,' he added, then glanced around the attic room and blinked several times as his eyes became more accustomed to the dim light in that part of the attic. 'Although I am surprised that you can see anything at all.'

He turned sideways and stumbled over a box of tools as he reached for the light switch but Ella was already on her feet and faster, and as their hands connected his mind and senses were filled with the image of the girl with her hair down he had seen in the garden that morning. The girl whose touch made the hairs on the back of his arm prickle to attention.

A hard fluorescent strip light crackled into life above his head creating hard shadows and dark corners. Ella instantly snatched her hand away as though she had been stung, but her pale blue eyes were still locked onto his. In this light the planes of her face were in hard contrast to her plump, soft-looking skin.

He was the first one to break eye contact and glance around the long narrow room where he had spent many happy hours exploring as a child.

'Wow,' he said. 'Well, this is going to be rather more of a challenge than I expected. It never used to be this messy.'

Ella found her voice. 'The roof was repaired last autumn. And then the designer needed somewhere to store all the bits and pieces he moved from downstairs. There are several families of mice living in the barn, and…'

She left the end of that sentence unsaid with a simple tilt of her head and Seb picked up on it. 'Everything ended up in here instead. Got it.'

Ella pointed to a large wooden crate with the name of a well-known champagne house on the side. 'That was the box where I found your mum's photo. There are a couple of photo albums in there mixed in with the other paperwork. It's too heavy for me to lug down those narrow stairs. I know there are more, but they've been pushed right to the back by the furniture.'

'Here. Let me pull them forward.'

'Are you sure?' Ella choked, flapping away the dust she was stirring up, which only seemed to make it worse. 'It's going to make a horrible mess on your clothes.'

Seb glanced down at his outfit and frowned. A designer-suit-and-bespoke-shoes combo was not perhaps the best choice for scrambling around in dirty attics, but seeing as he had not packed any casual clothes he didn't have a lot of options.

And he was on a mission.

A few items of damaged clothing were a small price to pay to find some clues to his personal history.

'I'll live,' he replied, trying to squeeze his way between unrecognisable lumps of old chairs and bookcases to reach the stack of boxes in the dark corner of the attic.

'Oh, no,' Ella exclaimed, reaching into the first box she had pulled forward. 'The frame is cracked. What a shame. I've often wondered why you didn't take these photos with you. I mean, if you didn't want them any more, you could have given them away to the rest of your family instead of leaving them here for the mice.'

Seb took the photograph from her and pressed his fingers onto the glass for a moment.

'When we left for Australia,' he replied in a low voice, 'I was allowed one suitcase and whatever I could carry in my rucksack. That was it.'

He tried to keep the hard reality of his dad's decision out of his tone but failed.

'I was twelve and leaving the only home I had ever known.' He looked up from the photograph and shrugged like the Frenchman that he always would be in his heart. 'I was far more worried about leaving my dogs and my pals behind to even think about the personal stuff, but…that was a long time ago.'

He carefully lowered the broken picture onto the pile of paperwork and photos and old birthday cards and goodness knew what else inside the wooden wine box.

'I'm actually surprised that this much has survived all of the tenants who lived here over the years. They mustn't have been very curious. Or there was nothing worth selling.'

When Ella didn't answer immediately he turned back to find her looking at him with a confused expression on her face.

'Actually there was only ever one tenant. A retired couple from Marseilles who only ever used the house during August. The house had been empty for over a year when Nicole and I moved in. Didn't you know?'

He stared at her hard, the words resonating inside his head before words burst out of his mouth from a place of anger and resentment. 'That can't be right. There was a family living here right until the day the divorce papers were signed.'

The hard words echoed around the small space, and the temperature seemed to drop several degrees.

Ella licked her lips, squeezed them hard together, crossed her arms and stretched up almost onto tiptoe so that she could stare Seb straight in the eye.

'Mr Castellano,' she said in a calm low voice, and her chin lifted another couple of inches. 'I may only be the housekeeper here, but I do not appreciate being called a liar.' She paused, took a breath then carried on, her shoulders lifting and falling as she spoke. 'So. Make your mind up. Do you want me to help you? Or not? Because if you do, you're going to have to change your tone. And fast. Have I made myself perfectly clear?'

Her lips formed a single line, her arms wrapped tighter across her chest and she just stood there, covered in dust and grubby marks, holding her ground and waiting for him to say something.

Seb responded by sitting down on the next box. Not caring about the damage to the fine fabric of his trousers or the indentations being poked into his skin.

It had been a very long time since anyone had dared to confront him face to face and ask—no, demand—that he change his tone.

His tone! His tone was just fine. It was his temper that was the problem.

She did not know what he had gone through. How could she? How could anyone understand when the only person who knew the truth was his dad? Luc Castellano was the person he should be challenging.

As for Ella Martinez? Ella Martinez was simply magnificent.

He had misjudged her. She had clearly been upset about a letter he had seen when he came into the attic, and perhaps that had made her oversensitive. The laid-back serene woman he had seen singing that morning had her own issues to deal with and he had no right to make them any worse by shifting his hot temper onto her shoulders.

Seb inhaled a deep breath, formed a thin-lipped and restrained smile and saw the tension in her jaw relax just a little.

'Quite right. You have made yourself very clear and I can assure you that I won't use that tone with you again.' He gave her a closed-mouth smile. 'I am pond scum. Please accept my sincere apology.'

Her lips twitched slightly, but he had already guessed that she was not going to let him off the hook that easily. 'What kind of pond scum?'

'Green slime.'

'Um. Okay.' She released her arms and leant back on one

of the chairs so that she was at about the same height as Seb. 'But I'll only accept your apology if you tell me why it was so hard for you to accept that this house had been standing empty. Because it really was. I know because I had to clean it!'

The power of her simple words combined with a steady and trusting gaze bored into his skull. She was telling the truth and he was the biggest idiot in the world. He had believed his dad. Suddenly he was tired of all the lies.

She deserved an explanation. No. More than that. She deserved the truth.

It had been years since he had felt the need to explain himself to anyone and Seb sniffed away the apprehension that came with finding himself in such an unusual position. Perhaps it was this house? The challenges just kept coming.

He had two choices. Stand up, walk out and jump into his car. Or stay and see it through.

Which was probably why he stretched out his long arms in front of him, hands palms together.

'I will tell you what I do know. I know that a few years ago I offered my dad a very large sum of money in exchange for this house at a time when he needed the cash to pay for his divorce and early retirement. I know that he refused to sell it to me at any price. When I asked him why, he told me that he had a sitting tenant who he had no intention of throwing out onto the street.'

Hot anger flushed at the back of his neck and his breathing raced. Pulling himself back, he added, 'So you can see that I was rather confused when Nicole was given the Mas as part of the divorce settlement a few weeks later. So, yes, I am somewhat annoyed.'

Then he twisted his mouth into a quirky grin. 'But that is my personal problem and I have to live with it. You do not. Hence my apology, Mrs Martinez.'

'Oh. Well, I find the direct approach works best.' Then her face brightened. 'Why don't you just call him up and ask him?'

Ask him? Ask him what? Ask him why he had lied about the fact that Seb's parents were not his real parents? Or perhaps ask him why he had married the first Frenchwoman he met in Sydney and expected Seb to make Nicole his new mother? And now this.

No, thanks. He had stopped asking and started making his own choices a long time ago.

'Maybe another time. Right now I'm far more interested in collecting together as much of my family history as I can before I leave today.'

'Well, in that case, you had better start with these photos of your parents' wedding.'

Ella pressed a leather photo album into his hands. 'Your mother looked so beautiful. She obviously loved being pregnant.'

CHAPTER SIX

Two hours later Seb was pacing the length of his bedroom and in danger of wearing a track on the surface of the fine wool rug.

He had not left the Mas Tournesol. He couldn't. He was far too agitated to drive anywhere except into the nearest solid brick wall or large tree.

The only good news was that he now had the answers to *two* of his questions.

He had not been adopted after all.

There was no doubt now that his mother had been pregnant when she married his dad. The wedding photographs Ella had found in the attic were wonderful—it was a delight to see his mother laughing and happy, surrounded by family and friends she loved. And without the huge bouquet of flowers to hide her baby bump, she was very definitely pregnant.

Ella had recognised the fact instantly when she had seen those photographs.

While he had been kept in the dark all of these years!

Okay. He could deal with that and stomping around his old bedroom was not going to help. It had always been a possibility that his mother had been in a previous relationship and it certainly did not change his deep connection to her.

Which left the missing piece of the puzzle. *Who was his father?*

And now he had a possible answer.

Because he had a name. *André Sebastien Morel.* Only this André was not a friend or some relative. André Morel had been his mother's fiancé.

Clutched in his left hand was a crinkled and faded clipping from a Montpellier newspaper he had unearthed from the second box of Castellano family records he had hauled down from the attic.

The edges of the clipping were torn because whoever had cut the announcement had used pinking shears from a young woman's sewing box.

The photograph in the living room had been taken at his mother's engagement party to celebrate her engagement to André Sebastien Morel some fourteen months before she married Luc Castellano.

There was no doubt. Both the date and the year on the newspaper clipping matched those on the photograph from the living room.

His mother had been engaged to André Sebastien Morel.

It did not mean that André was his father, of course, but it was a start.

Screwing up the ragged scrap of faded newsprint, he pushed it deep into his pocket, marched over to the window and clenched his hand over the narrow ledge, his fingers and knuckles white with the effort, desperate to breathe in some cool air.

He felt totally bewildered at the fury of questions and implications that showered out of this discovery.

There were two more boxes to sort through and the weight of what he might find there was starting to bear down heavily. He would do it. He had to.

But suddenly he felt constricted, trapped in this tiny room. He needed to walk some of this tension out of his body. And fast.

Perhaps a change of scene would help him to come up with a plan?

He needed to find out everything he could about André Morel. At the very least André had known his mother at a crucial time and could help track down his father. And at worst? His mother would not be the first girl to find herself pregnant and engaged to the man she loved—only to find herself a single mother. Either way, he needed to know.

Seb snatched up his carryon bag and started stuffing it with paperwork and photographs—but it was far too small.

The knock on the door startled him and he jogged the few steps to yank it open in frustration, only to find Ella peeking in towards him, carrying a small wooden tray complete with a white lacework napkin and a steaming beaker of the most delicious smelling coffee.

'Sorry to disturb you, but delving back into the past can be hard work. Do you need milk or sugar? I noticed you took your coffee straight at breakfast but I can always dive down and get you some. And how about a pastry? You look like you need a pastry. Oh. You're packing.'

The look on her face of simple interest and calm concern hit him like a bucket of cool fresh water, dousing out the flames of his anger and discontent.

She was gabbling. Nervous…for him.

The gesture was so genuine and caring that it grabbed him and shook him hard out of his grave state of mind.

He gently laid one hand on her arm and she stopped gushing and gabbling and looked at him. Really looked at him. As though she could see into his mind and untangle the turmoil of questions and answers that lay within. 'Are you okay?' she asked, the concern in her soft voice making it tremble.

The coffee was starting to slosh and the whole tray threatened to shake out of her hands so he carefully took it from her hands and lowered it onto a stack of old magazines. Almost instinctively his hands reached out to take hold of hers, but he caught them in time to push them firmly down into his trouser pockets.

'No. I'm not okay, and, yes, I am packing. Except that I am going to need several more bags,' he replied, his gaze on the assorted documents that were spread out all over the bedroom floor, close to Ella's feet.

Ella was wearing blue lace-up deck shoes and a green ribbon tied around her left ankle.

A small sigh escaped from her mouth and there was something about it that touched him. He barely knew her, but she was as transparent as glass. Which was probably why he startled both of them by looking into her blue eyes and asking, 'How about you? Are you okay?'

She breathed in through her nose and her chin tilted back a little as she rocked back on her heels.

'Been better,' she whispered, 'since you ask.'

Then her lips came together and for one, horrible moment that filled him with dread Seb thought that she was going to start crying on him.

Instead, she blinked several times as though clearing her mind, smiled and gestured with her head towards the corridor.

'It seems to me that you need a job to keep your mind busy. I need someone who is taller than I am and not frightened of heights. Yvette has gone home for the day and, to be perfectly honest, you look like you could use some fresh air. Interested?'

'You have a job for me?' He snorted in disbelief. 'I'm sorry, Ella, but I have more than enough on my mind right now.'

He flung his arm out over the jumble of papers and boxes. 'I need to get to the city and find myself a large conference table and a fast computer. Databases. Old newspapers. Anything that can give me the background data I need. Starting with my birth certificate. How do I get hold of a copy in a hurry? I've never seen an original.'

Ella peered around him at the crates. 'How do you know that you don't have one buried in those boxes that you have not opened yet?'

His eyes narrowed and he glared at her. 'I don't want to be rude but I need to get back to work. So if you'll excuse me, I'll finish packing. I'm sure there is someone else who can help you in the garden.'

She pursed her lips and watched him for a few seconds as he snatched up clothing and tried to cram it into the holdall. Without success.

Ella took advantage of a pause to step close enough for him to stop what he was doing and turn his head towards her.

'I'll trade you one hour of *my* time sorting through all of these boxes in exchange for one hour of *your* time in *Nicole's* garden. You do remember *Nicole*, don't you? She's the woman whose birthday party you are going to miss, even though you promised her that you would be here.'

Ella tilted up her head and twitched her button nose as she peered at the wedding photos Seb had spread out across his bedcover. 'Nice photos. Pity that you cannot spare a few days out of your *so* busy schedule to find out your family history. Or are you too busy making money to wonder who you really are?'

She glanced at her watch and folded her arms. 'But please make up your mind because I don't have all day.'

'Matt! How are you doing, mate? Having a great time by the pool?'

'Pool? I wish. I'm back in Paris,' Matt replied with a sigh. 'No rest for the wicked.'

Seb's eyebrows joined as his face darkened. 'What do you

mean, you're in Paris? Montpellier not exciting enough for you? Or is there a problem with the deal?'

'Nothing for you to worry about. The PSN Media lawyers need me to go over some fine details on the contract and it made sense for me to fly up to their offices. I'll be back on Sunday. Job done. Ready to sign the papers. Okay?'

Seb paused before swallowing down regret that his friend was not only out of town but also working on the deal while he had just wasted the last hour reading through farmhouse accounts and village sporting achievements. And failing to find a copy of his birth certificate.

'Do you need any help?' Seb offered. 'I don't want to be having all of the fun!'

'All taken care of. You enjoy yourself and I'll see you at the hotel Sunday evening. Then back home on Monday. Can't wait!'

A great whoosh of air jetted from Seb's lungs as Matt disconnected.

He still had to decide whether to stay an extra day and visit the local records office to get a copy of his birth certificate, or head back home with Matt. Even with Ella's help he had found little extra information in the photos and documents. Perhaps this was all a wild goose chase after all, brought on by lack of sleep and too much caffeine?

In the meantime he had to waste an hour doing gardening jobs for the woman he had barely spoken to since agreeing to accept her help.

She was infuriating! Especially when he could not argue with her common sense.

A deal was a deal. And he had lugged two boxes of paperwork back to the attic before calling it a day.

Seb strolled out into the warm sunshine and was greeted by birdsong and the sound of bees on the lavender and herbs in the kitchen garden.

A flash of colour appeared at the side of the house and he turned the corner just in time to see Ella trying to drag a set of very large, heavy ladders out of the barn, a basket hanging from the crook of her arm. From the huffing and puffing going on, the ladders were heavier than they looked, and Milou was playing around her legs at the same time.

'I had better help you with that before it falls on your foot and breaks some toes.'

'I can manage, thank you,' she blew out. Only at that moment her basket fell onto the patio as the ladder slipped and Ella veered towards it as her weight shifted. Seb ran forward and caught her arm just as she was about to lose her balance.

'So I can see. And when was the last time you pruned these trees?'

Ella raised her eyebrows and looked quizzically at Seb as he calmly took the ladder and opened it in one swift move.

'Hello! I am a London girl. Brought up above a jazz club! A window box was just about my limit. Yvette did prune the apples last winter but I can't remember her touching the cherries.'

Seb smiled and braced the ladders into a stable position against the trunk of the nearest cherry tree.

'If these are the original trees, I seem to remember that these cherries are good.'

'They are sweet. Dan loves them. And I'm hoping Nicole and her guests will too. At the moment my plan is to serve cherry frangipane tart as part of the dessert menu but I'm still fiddling with the recipe.' She took a sharp intake of breath. 'And there is no way you are going up that ladder in those shoes!'

Seb stopped and looked down at this black lace-up meeting-room leather designer wear.

'What's wrong with these shoes?'

'Nothing. They are excellent for a boardroom or fancy restaurant. But those leather soles are way too slippery to be safe. I hate to say it but I wouldn't be able to catch you if you fell. So...thank you for the help, but I'll take it from here.'

And before Seb could stop her, Ella had dived in front of him and was already skipping up the ladder. Until she reached three steps from the top and reached out towards the nearest branch, which was still way above her head. Then she stopped, dropped her arm, closed her eyes and clutched onto the wooden frame for dear life as the ladder slipped an inch, then another, before juddering onto a firmer spot. A very Anglo Saxon expletive escaped under her breath.

'Um,' Seb replied as she slumped forward onto the ladder. 'Good effort. Can you make it down?'

Her reply was a whimper and a gentle nod. 'I just need a minute,' she replied in a faint voice.

'Okay. I am going to put my hands on your waist. So don't be startled. It's just to hold you steady on the way down. Are you ready?'

Seb stood behind Ella and gently spread his hands both sides of her waist and pressed gently.

'I've got you now. One step at a time. Steady. That's it.'

A fast-beating heart pulsed below the fragile ribcage under his fingers. Fast like the caged finch he used to have as a boy. Only this was no bird. This was a soft and warm person trembling in his hands. A thin layer of fabric separated his fingertips from her skin and as she slowly extended one leg down to the next rung he breathed in a luscious smell of flowers and baking and the sweet fruit on the ground under his shoes and above his head.

He did not do intimate. And this was the closest he had come for longer than he cared to recall.

And he would have a lot of explaining to do if someone caught them like this, because, like it or not, when Ella reached the bottom of the ladder, she turned to face him. And leant forward with both palms flat against his chest, resting her forehead on the backs of her hands, so that he was looking down onto the top of her shiny brown hair as she caught her breath.

Connection. Deep, real and not to be denied. Connection and attraction. The kind of attraction that meant that he had no desire whatsoever to remove his hands from her waist.

Which was totally crazy!

He had felt unsettled earlier in the day when their hands had touched, but this felt deeper and more fundamental and so far out of his comfort zone it was not funny.

He swallowed down a moment of spiralling heat, then slowly released his hands from her waist and stepped back. Time to take control.

He was a tourist here with every intention of leaving at the first opportunity and he had better remember that fact. Perhaps he could find the time to take some lunch, but then he would be on his way. Job done.

'Are you okay?' he asked, looking into her face, and was rewarded with a hesitant smile.

'Much. Thank you. I, er, really should know my limitations, shouldn't I?'

'I'll trade you a basket of those cherries—' he pointed at the highest point on the tree, red with ripe glistening fruit '—for one of those tarts and that lunch you promised me. And I will be careful in my slippery shoes. Do we have a deal?'

Ella pushed out her lower lip and pretended to think about it for a second, then nodded and reached out to shake his hand once. The texture of her skin was dry. The palms calloused. A worker's hand. He liked that, which was bizarre. Perhaps he didn't like smooth-skinned girls with immaculate manicures as much as he thought he did? Either way, Ella was making his head spin.

'Deal.' She nodded firmly. 'I did promise you lunch. Provided you can do it now, of course. No time like the present.'

'Is that another of those English expressions you are so full of?'

'One for every occasion. Didn't you know?' Ella replied with a faint smile, her breathing back close to normal. 'I had better sort out that recipe. And don't forget that you owe me an hour. Best get to work!'

And with a wave of her hand she turned back towards the house, and Seb and Milou stood next to each other for a second watching the slim figure negotiate the patio.

Seb glanced down to see a pair of yellow eyes looking back at him.

'Well, we best get busy then, mate.'

There was a low sigh in disgusted response and the dog settled himself into comfort in the shade of the cherry trees.

'Good idea—you just stay there on guard duty! That's it. I'll do the work.' *And try and work out what I have just got myself into in more ways than one.*

An hour later, Ella looked out of the kitchen window at the sound of Milou barking.

Seb was pacing up and down the patio stones, wagging the fingers of his right hand and gritting his teeth while chatting away to someone on the cell phone.

Intrigued, she strolled outside just as he closed the call, drying her hand on the towel tucked into her apron waistband.

'Problem?'

He noticed her, and a slight flush of embarrassment flared on his neck, as though he had been caught doing something naughty.

The naughty Sebastien. Now that thought was enough to bring a smile to her face.

There were pieces of twig and dead leaves caught in the tight curls of his hair, his right forearm was scratched below his rolled up shirt sleeve and cherry juice was spotted all along one broad shoulder.

Strange how it suited him perfectly. The naughty Seb.

'The wasps,' he sighed. 'Took exception to my stealing their food. And my friend Matt has just found a legal technicality which will keep him in Paris until late Sunday. Looks like I am on my own.'

'Oh, thanks a lot! What a lovely compliment. Let me take a look at your sting.'

He held his hand above his head and gave her a look of disbelief.

'I can handle a wasp sting, thank you all the same. Even if it does smart.'

Ella raised both of her hands. 'I was simply going to offer you some antihistamine cream. But if you prefer to suffer in silence like a macho hero? Well, that's up to you.' She folded her arms and waited. Patiently.

He pursed his lips and sniffed. 'Antihistamine I can use. Pass it over.'

Ella gestured with her head toward the kitchen, unfolded her arms, then picked up the basket of cherries. 'Follow me.'

The first thing Seb saw when he walked into the kitchen were two family-sized open fruit tarts.

'Wow. You weren't joking. Are these a trial run for Nicole's party?'

'Partly for Nicole's party but I also need to get baking for the end of year fete at Dan's school this afternoon. I volunteered to help out with the entertainment. And most of the desserts! I made the fresh apricot and vanilla cream last week, but the cherry is a new recipe. The cherries I picked yesterday are so sweet and juicy it seems a shame to spoil the flavour with too much almond.'

Seb sat down in front of the two desserts which had already been cut into large segments. They smelt wonderful.

'Oh you mean the kermesse? Everyone loves the end of year party.' Seb smiled with a shake of the head as a long forgotten memory wafted into his mind. 'I vaguely remember dressing up as a tiger in primary school. Or was it a bear? I think we had too much fun running around in costumes to think about the food.'

'Then this could be your lucky day. I need a human taster to help me decide which of these two beauties would be best for a summer dessert. Think garden party on a hot evening. Think nice dresses and smart suits. No gloppy sauces allowed. The children and parents at the fete won't mind, but Nicole's guests might.'

Ella kept on talking as she loaded a plate with a large slice from each tart, slid it across the table towards him and popped the tube of antihistamine cream next to it.

'This is your lunch, so please help yourself while they are still warm. I know you won't hesitate to tell me the truth.'

Seb picked up the nearest fork and broke off a piece from the soft deep cherry tart. As he raised it towards his lips the overwhelming fragrance of sweet almonds, butter pastry and warm tart cherries had his mouth watering even before his lips closed around the food.

His eyes closed.

Wow. He was tasting summer.

Crisp pastry melted in his mouth as the rich ground almond paste soothed his tongue and, just when he thought it could not get any better, his teeth squeezed into a whole pitted cherry, and the warm juices burst onto his tongue.

It was the most amazing cherry tart he had ever eaten. No, the most amazing, delicious dessert he had ever eaten! Which was quite an achievement considering that he was on first-name terms with chefs at famous-name restaurants all over Australia.

He had been brought up to believe his grandmother was the finest cook in the world, but she had never made anything like this.

Seb flashed open his eyes and took another generous fork-load. Suddenly hungry for more. Just to make sure his senses weren't deceiving him.

As he bit into another cherry it took him back in an instant to the happy long days when he was a boy in this very kitchen.

Cherries, almonds, apples, apricots. Sitting in the garden on hot summer days, eating sun-warmed strawberries direct from the plants. Being scolded then hugged when he was caught with fruit-stained shorts and skin.

The flavours linked for ever in his mind and memory to this house and to this land. And the people who had made it special.

It was the taste of home cooking and fresh fruit. These days his meals tended to be fine food in hotel restaurants or a sandwich while he was working, but that was it.

When had he forgotten what real food tasted like?

Food made with love in a home with a family around the table.

It had been years since he had remembered so vividly what it had felt like to be part of a warm loving family. And it had taken a stranger to do it. A crazy Englishwoman had given him back that memory. And it meant a lot. Perhaps one day he would have a family of his own, but until then he was grateful for the memory.

Seb turned around in the chair to thank her just as Ella bent over from the waist to offer Milou a plate of what looked like broken pastry. The old dog almost jogged over from his water bowl to gobble up the crisp trimmings as Ella rubbed his head in tune with the wagging of his tail. For a few seconds woman and dog were framed in the sunlit doorway.

His eyes flashed up her long slim trousers to her trim waist and the sun-touched lower arms as she chatted to Milou, who had decided to try his luck by never leaving her side.

She looked happy. At home. Serene. Normal. And so very, very beautiful.

And the thought startled him so much that he coughed.

Beautiful? Where had that come from?

He instantly glanced away as the kettle came to the boil and tried to calm his breathing as he watched her stir the hot water into the ground coffee and savoured the delicious aroma.

God, this woman was good. Even the coffee was excellent.

His eyes moved to her left hand as she brought the coffee over to the table. The pale blue sapphires had no doubt been chosen to match the colour of her eyes by her late husband—whom she was probably still crazy about.

A tinge of something approaching jealousy sneaked into Seb's mind so quietly that he did not notice it until too late. Ridiculous!

One more reason to finish his packing and get back to his solitary life.

Ella looked up from Milou as he laughed out loud, and she sat down opposite Seb as she dried her hands.

'What's so funny? Don't you like it?'

He sat back in his hard wooden chair, hands behind his head, and stretched out, unaware that in doing so he had exposed a healthy section of bare midriff complete with muscular abs covered by a band of dark hair.

'Oh, please, not at this time of the day.' Ella covered her

eyes with one hand in dramatic horror. 'Put it away—it's putting me off my lunch.'

Seb glanced down, realised what she was referring to, and dropped his arms. For the first time in many years a flash of real embarrassment made him feel awkward and he busied himself pouring the coffee.

'Is there any place or time of day when it wouldn't be a problem?'

Had he really just said that out loud? Because for a second it sounded as though he was flirting—and he did not flirt. Ever.

'Well. Maybe there is.' Ella smiled closed-mouthed across the table as she accepted the coffee. 'But it usually involves swimming pools and drinks with umbrellas in them, and since we have neither…'

'I'll keep my shirt tucked. Got the message.'

He took a small sip of coffee, then sighed in pleasure.

'This is great coffee. Did you buy it around here?'

She shook her head.

'Montpellier. I'm pleased that you like it. Nicole finds it way too strong. And my parents prefer tea.'

Seb shuddered in response. 'I never got used to tea. Do you see your parents very often? Back in London?'

Ella took a long drink of coffee. 'No. They gave up their home in London years ago and bought one of those huge mobile homes. They're still working as jazz musicians and usually find gigs across Europe during the summer, then drive south for the winter. They pop in whenever they can.' She looked over his head towards the sunlit garden and smiled. 'But I wouldn't have it any other way. Especially for Dan.'

She glanced down at his plate, then looked up at him, her eyes dancing. 'You chose the cherry tart. What do you think?'

'Really delicious. And it would be perfect for a summer party. Nicole and her guests are going to love it.'

Ella slowly lowered her cup to the table. 'Good. Then you won't mind if I ask you a question?' She looked up into Seb's face, suddenly serious and full of understanding. 'Does Nicole know that you never had any intention of staying for her birthday party?'

Seb frowned. 'I knew that I was going to be in the area for a few days and we agreed to spend some time together for once. As it happened my business meeting was brought forward a week. I am sorry to have missed her, but there will be other times.'

'You do know that Nicole is my friend as well as my employer?' Ella replied. 'I hate to think that you are here to hurt her. Is it because of the divorce? Because I think she has suffered enough over that one.'

'No. It's nothing to do with that. I have every intention of apologising the first chance I get.'

Ella's focus was still on her coffee cup and when she replied her voice was cracked with sceptical concern. 'Then why are you still here, Seb? You were quite ready to leave this morning, but as soon as you saw your mum's portrait something changed. Can you tell me why that was? What did you find in that picture today that was so important to you?'

Seb paused before replying, her question resonating inside his head.

He had survived the traumatic events in his life by keeping everything personal bottled up inside himself. But here, in this kitchen, it somehow made perfect sense to give Ella the explanation she needed. And perhaps by talking through the issues out loud, he might make sense of them. Just as he had planned to do with Nicole.

This could be the only chance he would ever have to tell his story to a disconnected person and know that it would be heard sympathetically. Somehow, somewhere in the last day, he had found someone he could trust with his personal problems. And that was special.

Ella watched Seb's heavy dark eyebrows come together, his frown as deep as his heart.

She might have pushed him too far.

And in that instant she reached out and touched his hand and smiled to break the tension.

'I am the nosiest person in this town. Please excuse me.' Ella laughed. 'You are a guest in this house and your personal reasons for staying around are none of my business.'

In a moment she was on her feet, reaching out for the cups and plates and desperate to change the subject. 'Would you like to try the apricots before you leave? Yvette picked them at dawn.'

Only Seb caught her hand and kept it, calm and still. Something flicked across his face as though he was struggling to come to a decision.

'Six months ago my dad—' and at this Seb sighed a little too loudly '—had what the doctors described as a mini-stroke.'

She gasped and sat back down again. 'Oh, no. I'm so sorry. Is he okay?'

He nodded slowly. 'It was very small, and he was back on his feet in a few days.'

He looked up at her and his upper lip twitched. 'It shook me up, I can tell you. My job demands regular health checks, but nothing specific. Nothing where I needed a detailed family history and blood work.'

Seb's eyes were focused now on the palm of Ella's hand and he spread out her fingers, moving his fingertip along the life line on her palm before speaking again. 'I asked my company doctor to test me, in case there could be any hereditary problems. He's a friend. A good friend. So when he came to my office and closed the door behind him I knew it must be something serious.'

Ella thought that her own heart was going to stop. 'Oh, no. What did he say? Please?'

Seb meshed the fingers of one hand through hers as he resisted saying the words out loud.

'He said that I needed to talk to my dad. Because he had been through our blood work three times and there was no mistake. Luc Castellano cannot be my biological father.'

CHAPTER SEVEN

'WHAT did you do?' Ella whispered. 'I mean, that must have been a terrible shock.'

Seb nodded. 'It was. There were two options. I had either been adopted, or my mother had a relationship with someone else before she married my dad. Either way I knew that I had to ask my dad face to face and ask him to tell me the truth.'

'Of course! The wedding photographs! She was pregnant with you when she married.' Ella paused. 'But you didn't expect that, did you? What did he tell you?'

Seb sat back in the hard kitchen chair, arms stretched out on the table, but his fingers slid out from hers.

'I waited until dad was out of hospital and recovering back at home for a few days. He was feeling good and planning a holiday. And trying to pass his health problems off as just some minor problem. Anything to avoid the real issue.'

He made a rough chuckle in the back of his throat. 'As if I didn't know what he was up to. So I bypassed the chit-chat, showed him the lab-test results and mentioned the fact that I was old enough to hear the truth, and would rather hear it from him.'

Seb rose and started pacing the floor. When he turned back to Ella his face was dark, controlled anger only too visible.

'He told me to leave it alone. Water under the bridge. And he did not want to discuss it ever again.' He snorted and shook his head. 'I told him that I had no intention of leaving it alone. He told me that I was a stubborn fool and that I should get on with my life.'

Seb was holding onto the back of his chair so tightly that his knuckles were white in sharp contrast to the thunderous look on his face. 'And then we had a fight. I blamed him for taking me away from everything I loved to a country where I didn't even speak the language. He blamed me for driving Nicole away. And then it got worse.'

He flexed his fingers for a few seconds, trying to restore some of the circulation. 'I won't bore you with what happens when two Frenchmen start an argument where neither of them have any intention of backing down, but it was lucky that a couple of his friends turned up to play golf before things got out of hand.'

He shrugged. 'I admit it. I was angry. He had completely refused to answer any of my questions. So I told him he was a coward. His final words of comfort and consolation were along the lines of: "You can't bring her back," and then he slammed the door behind me. That was the last time we spoke.'

'Oh, Seb. That's horrible. You haven't spoken to him since?'

He raised his head and stared at her in disbelief. 'What would be the point of that? I know my dad. He won't change his mind. If I want to know who my father is then I'm going to have to find out on my own.'

'And that's why you want to follow up what you found today?' Ella raised her hands. 'Because he is right, you know. You'll have to decide what to do with any information you do find. There is a good chance that your father may not want to be part of your life, even if you want to be part of his.'

Seb nodded in agreement. 'I know it. There is a very real chance that André Morel let my mother down. But I don't want to make that judgement without knowing the facts. Perhaps she left him to be with my dad? It might help to explain his reaction.'

'Wait a moment. Did you say that his name was Morel?' Ella asked in a voice bright with curiosity.

Seb reached deep into his trouser back pocket and tugged out the newspaper clipping he had found that morning and passed it to Ella, who was now standing next to him as he looked out of the window into the garden where the trees were swaying wildly in the wind.

She scanned the few words, then let her shoulders drop. 'André Morel. Well, that cannot be a coincidence.'

Ella's hand slid down and her fingers clasped around Seb's, forcing him to glance down at the sudden sensation of her fingers on his as she spoke.

'I think that you had better come with me. There's something that you need to see!'

Ella half dragged Seb the few steps from the kitchen to the living room, then used her free hand to rummage around in a wicker basket of cards of all sorts.

'Mind telling me what I'm supposed to be looking at?' Seb asked impatiently as he tried to slip his hand away from hers, but she was not having any of it.

'This,' Ella replied, waving a party invitation in the air. 'I'm working this evening at my favourite hotel in town. Private birthday party for...wait for it: Madame Morel and family,' and she held the invitation behind her back. But Seb just scowled at her from his great height and lifted the card from her fingers.

'Is this for real? And what do you mean when you say that you are working at the hotel?'

'It is absolutely for real. And you may recall that my parents are professional musicians. Well, until I had Dan I earned my living as a performer. So tonight I am going to be playing and possibly singing for my supper and Madame Morel. *And—*' she shrugged her shoulders '—Sandrine told me that the Morel family are originally from Montpellier but have retired to their holiday home around here. I know that they *might* be a completely different family and it could lead to nothing, but isn't it worth taking the time to ask a few questions?'

'Maybe,' Seb replied hesitantly. 'And this is all going a little too fast for me to keep up. You are a professional musician working as a housekeeper, in the middle of nowhere. Is that right?'

'My choice. And no, I had not made the connection between the name Morel and your family until you mentioned it.'

Ella waited, watching his face, begging him to agree to follow this up. But patience was never her strong point, so she leapt in while he was still thinking about it.

'Come to the party tonight as my guest. I'll introduce you and tell the family that you are trying to trace an old friend. See what happens! There could be someone there who can put you in touch with this André Morel or may even have known your mother in person. You don't have anything to lose except a few hours in the city.'

Seb slid his hand from hers, and sank down onto the sofa. Ella perched next to him and brought her bare feet up onto the sofa cushions. Waiting.

Seb slowly raised his head to look up at the portrait of his mother before turning back to Ella.

'I can't be satisfied with the fact that my parents loved me.' He shook his head. 'That's just great. What an idiot, eh?'

Ella tapped her bottom lip a few times, then slapped her hand on the coffee table. Startled, Seb jumped forward.

'What?'

'Seb Castellano. I have a proposition for you.'

The surprised look on his face was replaced in an instant with a cunning smile.

'Oh? But we have only just met. I thought you English were so reserved!'

Ella smirked. 'Yes, very funny. You should be so lucky. This is serious. So please try and pay attention. Nicole Lambert has been a very good friend to me. I know how hurt she would be if I tell her that her stepson Sebastien, who she talks about constantly, had never intended to stay for her birthday celebrations in the first place—'

Seb sat forward but Ella gestured him back down with the flat of her hand. 'Please sit, I'm not finished yet.

'Okay. It goes like this. You stay here until next weekend and help Nicole celebrate turning sixty—which she totally hates the idea of, by the way—and in return…' She paused and breathed in through her nose. 'In return I will do everything I can to find out about this André Morel. I know everyone in this village and the hotel is the local meeting spot for the retired population who would love to have a detective job like this to work on. I can soon get the network going on tracking him down. What do you say?'

Seb reached out, grabbed her hand and kissed her knuckles before Ella could grab her hand back, if she wanted to. She didn't want to, and the natural wide grin on Seb's face said it all.

'I would say thank you for the offer, but I can't stay. I have to head back to Sydney on Monday, then Tokyo at the end of the week…what? Why are you shaking your head? Those tactics are not going to work on me.'

'You know, I never took you for a quitter, Sebastien Castellano.'

Seb bristled. 'Quite right. I'm not.'

'Then why are you making excuses? You know, Nicole

came back from Australia with a suitcase of photos of her amazing stepson. She was all alone in the world but she made sure she had your photos with her. How do you think she is going to feel when you leave the country before she gets back from holiday after…when was the last time you saw her, exactly? Two years? Three?'

Seb's scowl deepened. 'Three. We met at a charity concert in Sydney.'

Ella hugged her legs and rested her chin on her knees and smiled at Seb with such a sweet and innocent expression it was impossible for him to be angry with her. 'You know, I was explaining to Daniel on the way to school this morning how marvellous laptops and wireless Internet connections were. Some people work from home *all the time.* Without the need to travel at all.'

She shrugged and pretended to be examining her cerise toenail polish. 'Of course, after what you have just told me, I would understand if you feel compelled to travel to the other side of the world to talk to men in suits about computers instead of finding out who your real father is.'

Seb moved forward so that their heads were only inches apart. If he expected Ella to shuffle away as he moved into her personal space, he was thwarted because she did not budge.

'Monday. I'll stay until Monday.'

'Tuesday,' Ella retorted immediately. 'My final offer. But as an added incentive, we can start this very afternoon at Dan's school fete. All the parents will be there and there is bound to be *someone* who knows about the Morel family. *Then* you can go to the party. Just to make sure that we don't miss *any* possible leads.'

They looked at one another for a few seconds, the air between them crackling with electric tension.

But before Seb could open his mouth to reply, there was

an almighty crash from the kitchen and Ella leapt to her feet and sped down the corridor.

She slid to a halt at the door, hand on chest, so that Seb had to slide past and take in the damage.

Seb's laptop computer was lying face down on the hard tiles, surrounded by pieces of broken fruit tart, which Wolfie and Milou were gobbling up in delight.

'Oh, no,' Ella gasped in horror. 'I am so sorry. I should have closed the outside door. Bad Wolfie! Bad Milou! Is it broken? Please say that it is still working!'

Seb blew out a long breath and picked up the laptop and they both stared in silence at the smashed Wi-Fi attachment.

Ella cringed inside, and prepared herself for the onslaught! This was Seb's work! His precious laptop! She had totally blown it by being so careless. He had to leave now, whether she liked it or not. There was no way she would be able to convince him to stay and see Nicole now this had happened.

To her astonishment, he simply checked that the monitor and keyboard were still working in complete silence before turning back to her with a nod.

'It's okay. We build computers with cases designed to be pretty indestructible. Even against dogs and hard floors. I should be able to wire it into your telephone line through a modem. But my dongle is shattered.'

'I couldn't have put it better myself.'

'Slave driver! Have you seen my thumb? I may never type again. A few balloons you said. Nothing about 200 helium crocodiles.'

Seb waved his right hand in Ella's direction, but she was still luxuriating in the soft leather passenger seat with her eyes closed.

'Just part of the service,' she replied with a grin. 'Come to the Languedoc for wonderful new experiences. Thanks again for helping Dan with his pirate costume by the way. The eye patch idea was inspired. He looked terrific!'

She tipped her sunglasses higher and shuffled higher in her seat so that the light breeze lifted her hair down around her shoulders as Seb drove the open topped sports car along the quiet coast road.

'No problem,' Seb replied, smiling to himself, despite his frown. 'I had forgotten how much fun you can have at a school fete. I was actually in danger of enjoying myself a couple of times.'

'I noticed. You only answered your cell phone three times during the costume parade and you even put it away while you scoffed my quiche and salad. I take that as a compliment!'

'Oh more than that! I actually turned it off while you were playing piano at the old folks' home.'

'Wow!' Ella hissed. 'The school choir is not that good this year, but I did notice you charming the old ladies. You rogue.'

'Two of my school teachers actually remembered me! But not an Andre Morel. He was obviously not a local boy.'

'Oh, sorry. Even if that does explain the bright orange lipstick on both of your collars.'

'Oh, what?' Seb replied as he screwed his face up so that he could inspect his dress shirt, and then shrugged. 'It was worth it for the fringe benefits.'

'Oh? Do go on. Are you calling the bingo numbers tomorrow?'

He snorted a chuckle. 'I have the pleasure of escorting a pretty lady home while the young master of the house and his pirate crew are terrorizing the local cinema on a school outing. Even if the lady is taking me on a wild goose chase.

He started out at the countryside. 'Are you sure this is the right road?'

'And you a local boy!' Ella pointed to a signpost on

the deserted dusty road. 'Turn right here and all will be revealed.'

Seb frowned but gently swung the car down the single track road for a few minutes before the road ran out in a sand swept empty car park. The air was suddenly tangy with salt and the smell of the sea and as he swung out from the car his mind seemed to turn back the years with every caress of the wind on his cheeks.

They were deep in the Camargue. The huge flat plain of marshland and fresh and salt water ponds created by the river Rhone as it wound its way slowly to the sea over the centuries was laid out in front of him with only the sea in the distance.

Ella was already out of the car before he realised and automatically reached for his hand as though it was the most natural thing to do in the world, before dragging him through the rickety wooden gate and onto the loose sandy dyke which held back the water.

'Not a wild goose chase. A wild flamingo chase!'

And just as Seb was about to reply there was a low rustling and rhythmical beat of black and crimson wings above his head as five long necked flamingos flew across the tall grasses and landed perfectly in the shallow water with a quick back brake of soft pale pink wings. They honked and hooted as they flew, louder than geese, but so beautiful it took his breath away just to watch them.

Wild flamingos! *Flamants roses*!

Seb stood in silence with the warm sunshine on his face and watched the tall reeds sway in the sea breeze. Snowy white egrets and grey herons picked around the edge of the brackish pond, but it was the clusters of stunning flamingos feeding in the rich water on their red stick legs that captivated his attention. There were hundreds of flamingos just meters from the shore.

There was no sign of human life. No cars or houses. No laughing groups of primary school children having fun.

Simply sea, sky, birdsong and the rustle of tall grasses against the back of his hand.

And Ella. Captured in a moment in time with the wind in her hair and the sun on her skin.

Seb sucked in a breath to steady his heartbeat then exhaled slowly.

And it felt as though all of the tension that he had been holding in his clenched shoulders these past few months building up to the negotiations suddenly released all at once like smoke spiralling into the air.

His shoulders dropped away from his ears. The creases in his forehead relaxed away and the dull ache at the back of his head which had been bothering him since the long flight from Sydney simply drifted away on the warm tangy wind.

He would have been content to stand there for hours, but Ella released Seb's hand so that she could shuffle onto the warm sand and wrap her arms around her knees. Once in place she rested her chin on her hands and gazed in delight at the flocks of wading and flying birds on the pond.

Seb smiled down at Ella as she shirked off her pretty daisy sandals and squeezed her toes into the sand with a soft sigh of delight.

Then he glared at his dusty black business shoes and the tight black high socks which were digging into his calves below black business trousers. And felt totally ridiculous!

Without hesitating, Seb collapsed down on the sand, loosened his laces and shocked his bare feet by exposing them to the sunshine for the first time in months. He vaguely recalled the beach barbecue party he had set up for his design team in Sydney at New Year, but not the reason he had been called away at the last minute.

He wiggled his toes a few times to make up for lost time. It felt wonderful.

And then it hit him out of nowhere. Like a meteorite falling onto his head.

He had turned into a time poor cliché of a bloke who had all this money in the bank but no time to enjoy it!

How totally crazy was that!

It was so ridiculous that the laughter that burst through without warning came from a place deep inside his body, low in his abdomen. It was the kind of laughter that made his jaw ache for a few seconds before he was able to sniff and wipe his eyes.

Only then did he dare to turn his head towards Ella.

She smiled at him closed mouthed for a few seconds before shuffling over in silence then faced forwards so that they could both stare out at the flamingos, side by side and only inches apart. Their world encased in a cave of grasses and low shrubs.

Seb felt the sun and warm wind on his face and toes, and a strange sense of contentment and something close to joy filled his heart and his mind. Mingled with regret.

There had been a time when he loved to experience every new sensation with such pleasure and delight. When had he lost that ability?

And it had taken an English girl to help him to reconnect to this world free from high tech communications—and to make this moment something truly special.

'Sometimes I like to cycle down here out of season. Just to find some peace. I hope you don't mind?' Ella whispered.

He reached out for Ella's hand, raised it to his lips and grinned at her. Strange how he kept a tight hold of her hand and they sat huddled together in comfortable silence, just smiling. And she did not seem to mind at all.

* * *

'You could have warned me that I would have a reception committee,' Seb whispered to Ella as she hooked her arm around his and wound their way through the assembled guests towards the piano at the back of the room.

'What? And spoil the fun of seeing you charm the ladies?' She chuckled. 'You're quite the celebrity guest!'

Then she squeezed his arm a little tighter and joked, 'Sandrine has already ordered a fattened calf!'

Seb almost choked on his fizzy water. 'I'm hardly the prodigal son,' he spluttered.

'Um. I wouldn't be so sure about that,' Ella replied, dabbing with a napkin at the droplets of water he had sprayed onto the sleeve of his beautiful suit jacket. 'It was very kind of you to offer to take a look at Sandrine's Internet connection for her. I know she relies on those online bookings. It's not often they have a tame computer tech guru at hand.'

Before Seb could reply, Ella glanced over his shoulder and nodded. 'Speaking of shouting, I'm getting the nod from Sandrine. The buffet is about to be served, which is my cue to start work. I hope you like piano music!'

Ella slipped onto the piano stool and moved her hands swiftly up and down the keyboard, creating a stream of gentle lyrical sounds that seemed to Seb's untutored ear to be based around the melody of a familiar song but transformed under Ella's fingers into a tapestry of elegant and emotional music.

She might have told him that she had trained as a professional, but to his untrained ear she was superb!

'Are you improvising?' he asked in amazement.

She laughed out loud, but her focus remained on the keys. 'That's the whole point. Sandrine could have played a compact disc through the music system. My job is to create the background music which is special to this event.'

Ella raised her head for a second and nodded towards the

elegantly dressed lady who had greeted Sebastien so warmly after he had apologised for being a gatecrasher.

'The Morel family specifically asked for a combination of smooth jazz and some classical ballads from her favourite musical shows.'

Her hands slowed a little, the right hand picking out a theme he recognised from a very old Hollywood movie. Except that Ella was somehow playing the lyrics in the form of a musical expression so soft, smooth and warm that he was stunned by how every scrap of emotion was teased out in a few notes on a keyboard.

'You've done this before.' He smiled, and moved to the other side of the piano so that he could look at her face, suddenly delighted that he had agreed to come to this small hotel on a wild and windy evening.

Her nose wrinkled into a smile. 'Since I was about twelve. I love it, love it, and love it. Did I mention that I love it? I would play even if they did not pay me—but please do not mention that to anyone.'

Seb nodded sagely. 'Your secret is safe with me. But I do have one question. Why a cocktail pianist?'

'People watching, of course! Oh, you would be surprised what you see from behind a piano!'

She looked up over the lid of the piano towards the guests who were chatting away in clusters around the buffet table.

'After a while you merge into the background and that's when people reveal who they truly are.' She smiled up at him, then focused on a complex fast run up and down the keyboard using the lightest of touches. 'Any minute now, Madame Morel is going to make her way over and invite you to join her party at their table. Now, play nice! Who knows, by the end of the evening you may have discovered a whole *new* set of relatives!'

Sure enough, only seconds later Ella nodded and continued

playing as their hostess whisked Seb away. From her position, she could only sympathise as within minutes he was being introduced to the assorted aunts, uncles, cousins, nieces and nephews that made up the Morel family. And from what she could hear in random snatches, several of the men were either called André or had other Morel relatives by that name in Montpellier.

Poor Seb. This situation had to be bewildering for him.

As her hands moved through sequences of key strokes her muscles had learnt years ago, Ella glanced up from time to time.

Her eyes were drawn inexorably to the tall handsome man in the couture suit who had dominated the room from the moment he followed her inside.

Sandrine had taken one look at Seb and switched from being a professional hotelier of advanced years into a giggling schoolgirl who blushed at his every compliment.

Internet access! Sandrine! What a pathetic excuse. *The shame!* She was going to tease her friend mercilessly about that feeble excuse to keep Seb to herself for a few minutes.

It had given her just enough time to introduce herself to Madame Morel and her family and explain why there was an uninvited guest in the room. Who just happened to be the CEO of Castellano Tech.

Delighted did not come close!

Sebastien Castellano was at their little party and looking for one of the Morel family?

How exciting.

Make that *two* fatted calves, Sandrine.

As for Seb?

Sebastien Castellano had entered the room with all of the persona and confidence of someone used to achieving whatever they set out to do.

Plus he had two distinct advantages.

Firstly he had switched on his full-on charismatic charm offensive for anyone within speaking range. And then of course he was dressed for success. His dark suit was cut to perfectly emphasise broad shoulders and slim waist and hips—the same broad chest that she had pressed against so pathetically in the cherry orchard that morning.

Her fingers missed a key change and she quickly masked her error by turning the mistake into a jazzy flourish and carried on. That dazzling smile and those heart-stopping dark good looks had worked their power on more than Sandrine and their hostess!

The simple touch of his arm on hers had been enough to set her heart racing and head spinning. Despite her sweaty palms and dry mouth, she had managed to conceal her physical reaction to him…until now.

Working with Seb for the next few days until Nicole returned from holiday was going to be far more challenging than she had imagined.

From that very first moment when she caught sight of him sitting on the grass she had felt that certain, telltale, spine-tingling prickle of attraction that refused to go away.

Of course she had tried to rationalise it. She had seen his photos and imagined what Seb would be like in person. Meeting him, arguing with him, learning more about his reasons for coming home…that had simply helped her to understand the man himself.

Her fingers hammered out the dramatic phrasing from a powerful ballad.

Who was she kidding?

She was smitten.

Which was just about the silliest idea she had heard in a long time.

Looking at Seb now as he effortlessly worked the room,

the hopelessness of that attraction shook her by the shoulders like a good friend and demanded that she snap out of it.

He was a tourist who would be gone in a few days. Just passing through like a whirlwind destined to churn up everything in his path. Here was a man who only yesterday had no intention of keeping his promise to Nicole. Selfish perhaps? But also vulnerable when it came to his own family.

It was a powerful combination.

She was far too old to have a summer fling. Wasn't she?

Ella had been right. The gentle ebb and flow of the piano music blended seamlessly into the bright background chatter and laughter from around the room as Madame Morel introduced Sebastien to her extended family and friends.

Yes, there were several André Morels in the family, but André Sebastien Morel from about thirty years earlier? Cue puzzled faces and questions about places and dates he had few answers to. He had quickly accumulated a list of names and telephone numbers to follow up.

Friendly promises to ask around and get back to him mingled with the excellent food and drink to create a genuinely warm and welcoming sense of community and family.

His greatest challenge was refusing the delicious wine that a local winemaker had supplied for the evening. His apologies ended in a mass exodus of the men, and a few of the ladies, to the car park to admire his sports car. Only the howling cold wind prevented several test drives and they agreed to continue their heated debate on the relative merits of French and Italian motor manufacturers back in the warm comfort of the bar.

Where Seb had his first real opportunity to observe Ella as she worked.

The woman was a revelation! Just when he thought he was

starting to understand her, she came up with something even more remarkable!

The elf who had challenged him all morning had been replaced by an elegantly dressed beautiful woman with immaculate grooming.

Her dress was a shimmering blue silk cocktail gown with a matching gossamer wrap that drifted around her shoulders like candyfloss. The shade of the silk was a little darker than her eyes, but fitted perfectly onto her sweet rounded curves. It was an inspired choice. Elegant but not stuffy.

The bed hair was twisted up into a French chignon, leaving the smooth line of her neck clear for a small row of pearls.

Combined with natural looking make-up, which seemed to make her pale blue eyes sparkle even more than normal, the overall effect was stunning.

He had met and escorted many beautiful women and professional fashion models over the past few years whose artifice in making themselves attractive for the cameras evaporated a few hours later. Ella was a natural beauty, as easy in her own skin whether she was cycling along a country lane or baking in a country kitchen, or, now, elegant and sophisticated.

Ella Martinez the single mother, hard-working housekeeper and young widow was gone. Replaced by Ella Jayne Bailey. Solo pianist.

She simply took his breath away.

He was totally attracted to Ella Martinez and everything about her, and this new side of her personality and talent only added to his confused feelings.

Which meant that he was in deep trouble.

Seb gulped down the recognition of what he was thinking and feeling and quickly looked around the room to see if anyone had noticed him growing hot and heavy.

He did not do holiday romances, or short-term affairs.

But it did make him wonder about her choices.

What was Ella Bailey doing here in the middle of the Languedoc when she had so much talent?

Did she love her late husband so much that she wanted to hide away from the world with her son in the countryside? Perhaps she had wanted somewhere safe and secure where she could grieve in peace?

But perhaps it was more than that?

He leant against the wall as the other guests shuffled to the dessert trolley.

For now he was happy to watch the most beautiful woman in the room as her small hands moved effortlessly over the keys, her attention focused completely on the sound she was creating. Now and then her shoulders swayed from side to side with her head as she moved with the melody.

No sheet music. No written notes.

Yet the music soared into a tapestry of emotional, uplifting and inspirational sound.

This was her passion. Her delight.

He had always been fascinated by the work of skilled craftsmen, whether they were the expert cabinet makers who designed and made the dining-room furniture in his Sydney apartment, or the software engineers who saw their virtual designs take shape on mobile technology used around the world.

This was why every part of him knew that he was looking at a true artist.

Ella was superb. The music was perfect. *She was perfect.*

Except that she was playing the piano in a dim corner of the room, being ignored by the party guests as they chatted and sampled the delicious food. Guests like himself, for example.

He had been to so many parties and events over the years where there had been a cocktail pianist playing in the background, and, thinking about it now, he was shocked to recall that he had not once gone over to speak to the musician or even made a note of their name.

Ella was happy to stay in the background playing the piano while he worked the crowd for information about André Morel. In much the same way, Ella seemed happy to stay hidden away from the world in a remote farmhouse while he travelled the world!

His high-profile lifestyle would horrify Ella. What girl would want to have every aspect of her personal life and past history trawled through by journalists looking for a juicy headline?

And she was a single mother with a son.

Putting all of those aspects together, there was only one conclusion he could make.

He and Ella lived in completely different worlds with very different priorities and the sooner he realised that, the better. For both of their sakes.

Right now he had to focus. He needed to know a lot more about the Morel family before the evening was over.

Over an hour later, Seb was noting down the telephone number of an older lady whose cousin was called André Sebastien when he noticed that the music had stopped.

He calmly promised to call the next day, expressed his thanks, and then turned back to the piano.

Ella was standing now, her cell phone pressed firmly against one ear, her right hand squeezed against her mouth, and from the look on her face whatever she was hearing was not good news.

Seb instantly made his excuses and crossed the room to take her arm.

'What is it? Is everything all right?'

Ella shuddered and shrugged into her jacket. 'That was Yvette. She was reading to Dan when the lights went out. It has happened once before in a mistral and we lost power for a couple of days.' She clutched at Seb's arm. 'Can you take me home, please? I wouldn't normally leave a party before the guests but this is an emergency.'

'Sure. But I don't understand… Is it Dan? Is he frightened of the dark?'

Ella grabbed her bag, then pressed her hand onto her chest and took a breath. 'Not frightened of the dark. Terrified. I'm hoping that he will grow out of it, and I've tried everything but right now…he's going to be panicking. I need to get there and fast.'

'Of course. Let's go.' Seb grabbed her hand and led her through the hotel guests who were crowding in to chat about the music. Ella would have been lost in the crush but with Seb in the lead they were in the porch before Sandrine could reply to their quick 'farewells.'

Seb flung open the front door to the hotel and it was snatched immediately out of his hands by the gale-force winds that howled as loudly as the howls of protest from the hotel guests who were being buffeted by the freezing cold draught. By turning his shoulder to the wind, and protecting Ella as best he could with his body, Seb managed to shuffle their way across the car park and open the passenger door of his car for Ella, bracing it against his back long enough for her to throw herself into the seat before the wind slammed it closed.

By the time Seb collapsed into the driver's seat and pulled his door closed, he was freezing cold, exhausted and shaking with physical effort.

'I had forgotten what the mistral wind feels like!' Seb murmured to Ella, who had taken a firm grip with one hand on the grab handle on the car frame and was holding her seat belt extra tight with the other.

He slowly unclamped her hand from around her seat belt. 'Relax. You are surrounded by six air bags, Ella, and the same safety technology used in racing cars. You are quite safe.'

'Then why do you need six air bags?' she squeaked as the powerful engine roared into life.

'Not all drivers are as experienced as I am,' Seb replied with a hint of a smile on his lips, trying to reassure her, while thinking of some task to keep her mind busy. 'But I do need some help. Would you mind checking for fallen branches on the road? There is not much clearance between the road and our seats.'

Ella could only look ahead in terror as Seb carefully edged the car down the main road, the powerful headlights lighting up the thrashing trees and bushes either side of the road.

It was going to be a bumpy night.

CHAPTER EIGHT

ELLA came to a dead stop at the top of the staircase.

Dan was sitting huddled on the bed in his room, one arm wrapped tight around Milou's neck while his other hand was clasped firmly around the handle of their biggest torch.

The light was pointing upwards and reflecting from the ceiling so that the bottom half of his small face was white and the rest in shadow. Thick church candles burnt brightly inside glass flues, but their light was ineffectual compared to the giant electric torch.

The hard light contrasted so powerfully with his sweet striped pyjamas and towel dressing gown that her heart constricted with the sight of it. Dan had always been scared of the dark but she had not seen him looking so pale and terrified for a long time.

Ella forced herself to lift her head for the last few steps and skip lightly into Dan's room. She had to be positive for her son's sake—she just had to get him through the night.

'Hello. Are you still awake? This is exciting, isn't it? Did you hear the big wind? Oh—you found the torch from the kitchen! Good thinking.'

Ella flung herself down on the bed next to Dan and gave him an extra warm cuddle.

'What a clever boy you are. And thank you for helping Yvette.'

'I had to help find the torch,' he finally managed to reply. 'But then the wind got a bit scary.'

'Well, seeing as you have been so brave, I think you can come downstairs for a few minutes and tell Seb all about the excitement.'

In an instant Dan was shrugging the duvet from his legs and sliding out of bed.

Ella grabbed hold of his hand and used the torch to guide their way to the hall, which was flooded with light from the driveway. Yvette had already driven off home, but Seb had left his car headlights on so that the powerful beams pointed straight onto the house and the glass panel above the front door.

She could have kissed him on the spot.

An even brighter light came walking out of the living room—the beam so powerful that Ella shaded her eyes.

'Hey, guys. Hope you don't mind that I lit the fire. And what do you think of this new torch? Cool, eh?'

Dan shone his torch onto the carpet, then looked at Seb. 'Yours is better than mine,' he said with a quivering-lip voice. He looked back and forth between the two torches and said, 'I need one like that.'

'Well, how about a swap? Here, try it out. I should warn you, though. It's pretty heavy!'

Dan ran forwards to take the handle from Seb, then blew out hard. 'Really heavy!' Then he started waving it about. 'Look, Mum. Now I can see everything.'

'That's wonderful. In that case you can guide our way to the kitchen. I fancy some hot chocolate. And you'll never guess what happened to me tonight?'

Dan lifted his head towards her, eyes wide and suddenly curious.

'Did your lights go out too?'

'No, they didn't. But Seb gave me a scary ride home in his sports car. What do you think of that?'

'Hey! It wasn't that bad! I didn't go *that* fast.' Seb laughed and winked at Dan, whose mouth curled up into a grin. But as Seb strolled down the short corridor, Ella realised that it was Seb's fingers Dan sought rather than hers, his tiny hand engulfed inside Seb's palm.

And it broke her.

Hours later, Dan's head lolled on Seb's shoulder as Seb carried him back to his toy-filled bedroom, with Ella carrying the torch to guide their way up the narrow old staircase.

They had shared hot chocolate made in a pan on a gas ring fed by a bottle of propane, then huddled in front of a roaring fire in the living room. Seb had drawn the heavy curtains, but nothing could block the howling wind on the other side of the glass and the draughts that blew the smoke right back down the chimney, making them all choke and splutter and laugh.

Dan had been given the task of holding the big torch while Seb fed the fire and lit a cluster of scented candles so they could see where the cups of hot chocolate were.

It had seemed only natural for Seb to divert Dan with stories about the hot and dusty places he had visited and all of the exotic plants and birds that he had seen during the previous month in the North of Australia.

Tales of kangaroos and Koala bears and kookaburras and remote towns where people had to drive for hours before they saw another house or person.

Places where people needed computers and clever phones to keep in touch, and even go to school. Places where the software and communication systems that his company made came into their own.

An hour later Dan was cuddled against Milou and his

mother on the couch, half asleep and yawning his head off, despite calls for more stories about the kangaroos.

Seb lowered Dan slowly onto his warm bed as Ella held back the quilt, and then tucked him in.

'Doors, Mum. The doors.'

Dan's eyes fluttered open and Seb turned away as Ella opened up the big wardrobe door and shone the powerful torch inside so Dan could see the neat shelves of clothes and toys.

And absolutely no monsters.

Ella bent over to kiss Dan, wish him goodnight, and stepped quietly onto the landing.

Just as Seb went to follow on, Milou tried to jump onto the bed, but was not quite up to it without Dan helping him up, so Seb did the honours instead, and as he did so Dan tugged at his sleeve. 'Have you looked inside? Over there? Cause I can't see over there. I don't want to worry Mummy.'

Seb glared at the dark spot next to the cabinet, reached out and turned on the powerful torch from the car, grateful beyond measure that the batteries were new and unused.

The whole bedroom flooded with light and Dan peered out over the top of the bedcovers before snuggling down again with a sigh of contentment.

Seb popped the torch onto the bedside table. Just in case Dan needed it again.

Then without thinking or hesitating, he whispered, 'Night, Dan. Sleep well.'

And a sweet child's voice answered, 'Night, Seb.'

The living room was still cold despite the fire, which had started to ebb down, and Seb quickly tossed dry wood onto the burning embers.

'I suppose power cuts are one of the downsides of living

in a remote farmhouse. Some things clearly haven't changed,' he said in a positive voice, then looked around for Ella.

He was shocked to see a tearful, anxious little face staring back at him, her skin pale even in the warm amber glow from the fire.

Ella had wrapped an old patchwork quilt around her shoulders and was sitting hunched up with her knees to her chest, hugging the quilt tight around her body.

She looked cold, shivery and terrifyingly, achingly sad and empty. As though all of the joy had been drained out of her. When she spoke she asked him the most ridiculous question he had ever heard.

'Am I a bad mother, Seb?'

He was so shocked that instead of answering he simply turned back to the fire to hide his own rush of emotions, stoking up the wood into bright flames.

Seb did not have to look at her. Her anguish was only too clear in her voice. The type of anguish that no bland denials and complacent phrases could eradicate.

'I love Dan so much and want him to be happy,' Ella continued in a low tremulous voice, 'but maybe Christobal's parents are right? Maybe I should move back to Barcelona? He will have a better education and money and... He would never have to worry about the lights going out in a storm and being scared again.' She paused for a second before her voice faltered in a few halting words. 'He was so frightened! I don't want him to be scared. *Not ever.*'

She was crying now, the tears running down her cheeks as she fought and lost the battle to hold back her fears and regrets.

Which was why Seb did the only thing he could do. He sat down next to her on the sofa and wrapped his arm around her shaking shoulders, gathering her close to his side so that she was cuddled all along the side of his body, cocooned inside the quilt.

The contrast between the Ella he was holding and the Ella who had been playing and laughing only a few hours earlier was so sharp that Seb took a moment to close his eyes and try and clear his head. He revelled in the glorious sensation of holding her in his arms, but immediately felt guilty for taking advantage of her sudden vulnerability.

His chin pressed onto the top of her hair and he hugged her closer, wrapping the quilt around her back, desperate to share his warmth with her. Her perfume was fainter now, mingled with the soft fragrance of lavender from the quilt and Ella's own sweet scent. Unique, powerful and totally compelling. A scent that pulled him in so fiercely that he never wanted to let her go.

She snuggled closer. Just a tiny inch. And his heart soared in delight. It had been so long since he had been in such close physical contact that the gentle thump of her heartbeat inside the ribcage beneath his hands seemed magnified. Loud and fervent.

He did not do intimate. Ever. Yet here he was, holding this wonderful, amazing woman while a little boy slept above them. How had that happened?

They barely knew each other and yet he felt so connected. Perhaps it was this house? These four walls, now cast in deep shadows, which made the rest of his life suddenly come into sharp focus.

Or was he simply in the right place at the right time to offer her some comfort? Any port in a storm? No. It did not feel that way at all. This was real. And so was her concern.

Seb slowly pressed his cheek to her hair before speaking in a low and soft voice.

'I've only been here for one whole day but I already know that Dan is a very, very lucky boy. You have given him so much more than any amount of money can buy. He's a remarkable young man. You should be proud of your son…' and at this point he lifted some strands of her hair behind her ear '…and what you have achieved.'

Seb slid slightly to one side and tilted her chin up towards him, only to find her looking up at him, her eyes focused on his in the flickering firelight, as though seeking the confirmation that the words were real and for her.

He raised his right hand and his palm cupped her chin as he gently wiped away the trace of a tear from her face with his thumb. Her skin was soft and her colour was already starting to return, bringing a flush of life to her cheeks.

'You are a remarkable and wonderful mother, Ella. Don't let anyone *ever* tell you any different. Okay?'

He looked into her eyes now, and felt her chest rise a little under the quilt.

Seb tried to ignore the overwhelming urge that swelled from deep within him to caress and protect her—an urge that was threatening to break down his resolve not to become even more connected to Ella.

Except at that moment Ella seemed to take his uncomfortable squirming as a signal that she could move to a better position so that she could argue with him, and made an effort to wriggle out of her quilt. He recalled the dress that she was wearing and decided that it would be better for both of them if she stayed wrapped inside her quilt, so he held her even tighter against his body until she conceded.

'Okay,' she whispered, and her mouth curved up at the sides into a timid smile that was so warm, trusting and caring that any shade of doubt he might have had was blown away in a fierce blast of red-hot attraction.

Only this time it was Ella who surprised him by wriggling her left arm free on top of the quilt and laying it on his chest as she snuggled closer into his shoulder and gave a gentle sigh.

A sigh of contentment that hit him hard and hit him again as his own body responded to her touch.

His heart raced to match hers, the blood hot in his veins. The gentle pressure of the side of her face on his chest flicked on switches he'd thought were long burnt out. Switches connected to a tangled set of wires labelled with words like trust and caring and commitment.

Caring? His mind reeled at the very concept. This was impossible. Ridiculous! He could not be falling for this lovely woman he first met only yesterday. He just couldn't! Could he?

What about the small matter of the fact that the worlds they inhabited were not only continents apart, but her world was based around Dan and the simple life in this house, whereas his…? He had renounced love and chosen the type of frenetic lifestyle where no second of the day was wasted in relaxation.

They might be breathing the same air, but apart from that they had so little in common it was crazy.

He glanced down at the gentle rise and fall of her chest against his in the warm glow from the now-hot fire. She was dozing. This beautiful, fragile, clever and funny woman was using him as a pillow.

And he absolutely adored it.

He was doomed.

And where did that leave him? Leave all three of them?

Only one way to find out.

'I don't know how to say this, so I'm simply going to say it anyway.'

His jaw seemed to tighten and as she looked into those wonderful amber-brown eyes they smiled back at her as though he was looking for reassurance that what he was about to say would not be rejected.

'You are a very attractive woman, Ella Bailey Martinez. The kind of woman a guy like me could fall for very easily. And cause a lot of damage in the process.'

His hand slowly lifted up her fingers to his mouth, and his warm lips pressed against each of her fingertips, one by one, sending delicious shivers of tender longing sweeping through her.

It was the sweetest tender touch she had been missing, and the instant Seb lowered her hand and released her fingers she knew that she wanted him to do it again. And again.

It had been so long since she had been held like this, touched and caressed like this, even before Chris died when their love life had died down to the point of a few absent-minded pecks on the cheek when he remembered.

There had been nobody else since.

Seb was like water in a desert. And she wanted to drink her fill.

'I need to know if you feel the same way,' he asked. 'Or is it only me?'

She had sensed the attraction since the moment they had met on the dusty road, but putting it into words was harder than she expected.

He needed her to tell him how she felt.

He *needed* her.

And it was terrifying. What was going to happen? Was it possible that they could have a future together? Could she let this man into her life and take the consequences? For herself and for Dan?

Yes, Seb had been kind to Dan, and she had been surprised that her little boy had taken to Seb so quickly, but her simple life in rural France was poles apart from Seb's high-flying world.

What had her mother always said when she struggled to

learn how to sing a new ballad? 'Go with your heart first. Follow your heart.'

Her fingers stroked his cheek and his eyes fluttered in pleasure before opening with such desire that every cell in her body screamed, *'This one. Choose this one.'*

She grinned and lifted her shoulders into a slight shrug. 'I'm scared.'

Seb must have been holding his breath because he shuddered out a half-smile before hugging her closer. 'Me too.' His hand caressed her waist and she sensed the air change a little before he braced himself with the big question. 'Are you scared for Dan? Or is it Dan's father?'

She closed her eyes. She'd never talked about Christobal to anyone. Certainly not to Nicole or Sandrine. As far as they knew she had been a devoted wife who was still mourning the loss of her soulmate. The truth was too hard. And way too difficult.

Only now that she tried to recall the personal conversations with Seb in the short time she had known him, she realised that her husband had never come up. Seb had no way of understanding how she felt about the man she had loved once.

Her stomach cramped in anxiety and he instantly seemed to sense her resistance.

'You don't have to talk if you don't want to. Being a single mother is hard enough. I know that Dan has to come first in your life.'

Now he was being sympathetic! This was totally wrong. She did not want sympathy from Seb. Just the opposite. And she especially did not want him to think that memories of Chris were still influencing her choices.

'No. It's okay. After Chris died in a car crash, my life was in turmoil.' Ella focused on a spot in the pattern of the patchwork quilt as Seb squeezed her hand once more in encouragement. 'But you know the hardest part? I knew that

I was lying to myself and everybody else. Christobal and I were so in love when we married. It was a magical time for both of us, and I will never forget it. He was really making a name for himself as a conductor around the world and I loved travelling with him to rehearsals.' She flashed a smile at Seb before refocusing on moving her hands in his.

Her head fell onto Seb's chest. 'Only… Once I got pregnant I couldn't go with him on long overseas tours, and we…we drifted apart.'

Ella sucked in a breath and concentrated on the sound of the crackling fire and Seb's heart beating under his shirt to steady herself enough to go on.

'Chris adored Dan and we both agreed that he had to come first. We were both professionals. We had no illusions about how hard it was going to be when he was away so much. We just didn't expect our marriage to fall apart so completely and so quickly in the process. The truth is…' And her voice faltered, before she steadied herself to explain, 'The truth is that for the last two years of marriage we were living more like brother and sister.'

Her head lifted in emphasis. 'Oh, we cared about each other. Very much! And he loved Dan! We never stopped being friends, and I think we made a good show of pretending to be a happy couple, but in private we both knew that our marriage was over.'

Seb kissed her forehead before replying, 'I am so sorry.'

She sighed and nodded once. 'Me too. Christobal was a wonderful man who had a brilliant future ahead of him, and I still mourn him and miss having him in my life. Only, not so much as my husband, but more like the best kind of brother a girl could wish for. He was great company. Funny. Talented. He was the best friend I ever had. I miss him every day.'

'I don't understand. You are still wearing your wedding ring and answering to your married name,' Seb replied, and

Ella could feel a new awkwardness between them and he moved slightly back on the sofa, creating a physical as well as a mental barrier.

'I was proud that he chose me as his wife and the mother of his child. As for now?' Ella shook her head. 'People know me as a grieving young widow and my efforts at making a new life haven't gone too well, so I let them believe it for Dan's sake as well as mine. I hate being such a hypocrite.'

'You have nothing to be ashamed about,' Seb replied, his brows coming together into a frown. 'People change. It doesn't mean that you didn't care about each other or your son.'

'I feel more disappointment than shame. I knew all about touring! How hard a life it was! But I believed that we would have a marriage like my parents. They have been married thirty-five years and are still so much in love it hurts. They can't bear to be separated.'

Tears started to prick the back of Ella's eyes now, and she straightened her back on the sofa and tried to slide away, but Seb brought his legs up, blocking her escape.

'I'm right here. And I'm not going anywhere until you get those demons off your chest.'

'What if I don't want to talk about it?' Ella replied, her voice bumbling with more indignation and frustration than she had intended. 'I'm not proud of having a failed marriage. And I'm even less proud of pretending to the world that it was perfect. Because it wasn't at the end.'

'You shared a wonderful few years together. Is that right? Is that true?'

She hesitated, already sensing where Seb was going with this question. For years she had felt the pain of never knowing what might have happened if Christobal had not jumped into that *particular* taxi cab on that *particular* day. Her feelings were so mixed up. Guilt. Regret. Disappointment. And fear. But one thing she was clear about was the answer to that question. She had loved Christobal and for a precious time he had loved her. 'Yes. Yes, that is true.'

Seb slipped off the sofa and leant on the rug in front of the fire so that he was facing her directly. 'Then celebrate that fact. And move on.'

Her mouth dropped open. 'Move on? How do you propose I do that when I have a six-year-old little boy to take care of? If you want to feel sorry for someone, save your sympathy for Dan. He is the one who will never know his dad!'

She was shaking now, her voice harsh and angry despite being little more than a whisper. 'Dan needs me to be strong for him. I'm all he has.'

Seb reached forward and clasped her hands in his, before she could move them out of reach. 'How old was Dan when his father died?'

Ella looked into Seb's eyes and the tenderness and caring in them almost broke her. 'Eighteen months. No more than a baby really. We were living in Barcelona with his parents back then. Chris was in Mexico on tour when his taxi was broadsided by a truck. No brakes. He died instantly.'

A photo of the crash flashed into her mind and she instantly closed her eyes and squeezed them together to block out the terrible images, suddenly angry with Seb for making her see it again. For taking her back to those dark days of oblivion and pain when she was so very, very alone.

'It must have been horrible for the whole family. His poor parents!'

'Oh, yes, his poor parents!' Ella replied with so much venom in her voice that she pulled her hand away from Seb's grasp and slapped it over her mouth.

Horrified by what she had said, Ella spun her legs over the edge of the sofa and tried to stand, only to fall back dizzily, light-headed, her heart pounding.

Instantly Seb was holding her upright in his arms,

supporting the back of her head with one hand as his other held her firmly against him, close enough for her sobs to be soaked up by the fabric of his shirt.

'Oh, that was so unfair! Please forget I just said that. I am a horrible person for even thinking that way!'

'No.' Seb's reply was muffled by her hair. 'You are not a horrible person. Far from it. But something happened to upset you. You have come this far, Ella. You can tell me. Why is there such a rift between you and the Martinez family?'

Ella felt Seb lift up her chin so that she could see him smile down at her as his hand caressed her lower back, holding her in his arms, taking her weight. Supporting her. Those strong arms giving her the strength she needed to tell him the truth.

'They…' And she swallowed down hard and clamped her eyes shut as she clutched Seb even closer. 'They tried to take Dan away from me. And they almost succeeded.'

CHAPTER NINE

SEB pulled the collar of Ella's fleece jacket a little higher to ward off the chill wind that was still howling outside the kitchen door. The skin at the back of his fingers lingered just a little too long at the base of her neck as he flicked the hair from under the collar and smoothed down the soft, cosy fabric.

And he sealed it with a gentle touch of his lips to the hollow just below her ear.

His reward was a smile as warm as the steaming tea he set before her on the kitchen table. A ring of beeswax candles lit up the centre of the kitchen, their flickering flames creating an intimate dome of light, just bright enough to light the gas ring without accidents.

'You don't need to tell me anything else, Ella. I know that you are a wonderful mother. You've made a life for yourself and Dan. That's all that matters.'

Ella nodded and sipped her tea. 'That's true. But it's okay, I want to tell you.' She looked at him with such trust and innocence that he slid back onto his seat and waited for her to begin.

The confident and joyous woman he had admired only a few hours ago was starting to return. And if telling him the truth made it easier, then he would listen. 'I haven't talked about this to anyone. Not even Nicole or Sandrine. But I have to go back to Barcelona with Dan next week, and maybe it is time to sort out what happens to Dan in the future.'

She sighed once, then gritted her teeth as painful memories hit hard.

'After Chris died in the accident…well, I was a mess, Seb. So when Chris's parents offered me a home with them for as long as I wanted, I was truly grateful. I really was. Everything was such a blur. My parents came to Barcelona for a few weeks but they had already given up the jazz club in London and bought a motor home to help with their touring. It was not designed for a young baby. As the months went by I started to feel…I don't know. Trapped, I suppose. I like Barcelona, it is a beautiful city with a wonderful live music scene. But that made me yearn so much for my old life on the stage.'

'And perhaps a little desperate to get your life back on track?' Seb added, wanting her to know that he understood, only too well, how it felt when your world was turned upside down because of events you felt powerless to control.

She shrugged. 'I did something stupid, and booked a gig at one of the local jazz festivals Chris and I used to go to together with our musician friends. It was just a couple of hours on a lovely July afternoon.' Then a smile crept back onto her mouth and Seb realised just how much he had missed that. 'Dan slept through the whole thing at the side of the stage under the fierce protection of my Spanish friend and her mother.'

Ella closed her eyes and her smile dropped. 'The fallout was horrendous. I was accused of being irresponsible and, well, a poor mother, for taking an infant into that sort of environment. I tried to explain that he had the best babysitters in the city *and* I could see him the whole time, but it was no good. As far as they were concerned I could not be trusted to look after their grandson.'

Her hands clamped tight around the beaker of steaming tea. 'So they called their lawyers. Who took me to the cleaners.'

Ella focused on the flickering shadows from the candlelight and her voice was harsh now. 'You can imagine the kind of picture their lawyers painted.'

She sighed and half smiled up at Seb. 'Until I got married I had basically lived most of my life as a nomad. Apart from a few years of formal education in London I had been educated and had grown up on the road. Touring from town to town. Making a living as we went.'

She lifted her hands and pointed from finger to finger. 'I don't have any formal qualifications, even if I do speak several languages and can sight-read, play and sing just about any piece of music first pass. No savings, of course. No pension. No insurance. And no way of earning a living to support myself and my son. Oh—and I had no home to go to.'

She dropped her hands onto her lap. 'Put that all together and any judge is going to think very hard about whether the child's grandparents should have custody instead of this flakey, messed-up girl sitting in front of him.'

Seb took her hands in his so that their faces were only inches apart.

'What did you do to change their minds?'

A warm and coy smile beamed back at him. 'I did something I had never done before. I fought back. It was tough.' She snorted. 'Make that very tough. My parents helped with professional references and somehow I managed to convince them that I could support myself without handouts. But it was still hard.'

She looked down at Seb's hands and turned them over so that she could trace the life line across his palm with a fingertip. He sucked in air as delicious shivers moved up his arm and into the part of his heart he had thought was closed off from the world and all it had to throw at him—closed off with the barriers of work and a relentless drive to succeed.

Now this seriously amazing little woman was doing a pretty good job of tearing them down.

'I didn't blame them, you know. I've never blamed them. They had lost their son and wanted the best for Dan. Or maybe that was the best for them at the same time. I don't know, but it was all about Dan in the end.'

'And what about you, Ella? Are you saying that they wanted Dan to grow up in an ivory castle without his mother?'

'Maybe. But I understand why his parents did it. Never more so. It just took me a few years to catch on.'

'Are you justifying what they did?'

'No.' She shook her head. Her voice lowered an octave. 'Focusing on what was best for Dan made me grow up in a hurry. Suddenly I had to prove to the local authorities that I had the ability to take care of a child on my own and pay the bills. A safe home. School. Medical care. That meant a regular income from a full-time job. Maybe even a bank account with some money in it.'

She bared her teeth in a grimace. 'That would be new. Believe me. Pensions and savings were for other people who had regular jobs.'

'You didn't have any savings at all?'

Ella shook her head then blew out, hard.

'They were the hardest six months of my life but eventually I left Barcelona a different person from the girl who was going to sing every night of the week just for the love of it, to please myself and my family, then move on to the next venue. I had changed. A lot.' She paused and her eyes flicked up at Seb as he held his breath for what she was about to say next.

'I had gone from being a girl who was always ready to take off for the next thrill at a minute's notice to a single mother who was at home with a child who was going to get all of my attention if I wanted to keep him. I had to find a job. And fast.'

'And then you met Nicole.'

She nodded. 'Actually I met one of Nicole's friends at the Avignon Jazz Festival. My parents had a three-set gig so I brought Dan on the train from Barcelona. She asked me if I knew anyone who might be interested in working as a housekeeper for her friend who had a holiday home. Ta da! I loved to cook. I could learn to clean. Two days later I had a roof over our heads and a regular income. And we never went back.'

She blew out dramatically and dropped her head back. 'And there you have it. A brief introduction to the life and times of Ella Jayne Bailey Martinez.'

Her head came back up and she squeezed Seb's hands. 'I am so sorry. I never intended to bore you silly. Can I blame it on the mistral? It does make some people melancholy.'

'And perhaps a little scared about what the future might hold?'

Ella bit her lip and swallowed, her face quiet and still, but her eyes were on fire.

'I'll remember the good times Chris and I shared together but I can't control the past. Only the future.' And she smiled at him. A smile that lit up her eyes and mouth and face. 'Right?'

'Absolutely. Does that mean you might be ready to go on your first dinner date in…how long has it been? Over four years? Well, that just has to be wrong!'

He took one look at the stunned expression on her face and grinned. 'I understand that there is some form of music festival in the area at the moment. I will be out for most of the day in Montpellier following up a few leads on André Morel, but I was wondering if you would care to join me tomorrow evening? Oh. Sorry, later *this* evening for some dinner and musical entertainment? It sounds like a fine excuse to start looking forward instead of backwards, and possibly even enjoy yourself.'

'You want to take me out to dinner?' She squeezed her eyes half closed. 'No. Not if it is out of pity for the sob story you just squeezed out of me. Is it?'

Then he tapped her gently on the underside of her chin with his knuckles.

'It's been a long time for me too, Ella.' His voice was gentle and warm. 'But now I'm asking you to trust me. Can you try and do that? Trust me as much as I want to be with you?'

And before Ella had a chance to answer he shifted his head and brushed her lips with his, the tip of this tongue moistening her soft mouth. Begging her to respond as he moved slowly to her chin and neck, kissing her soft skin with all of the tenderness his heart could bring. Desperate not to break the deep connection he knew bonded them together.

His mouth brushed along the length of her cheek, the stubble on his chin rough against the soft warmth of her skin, and tasted the salt of dried tears.

Drawing back, he gazed at her in wonder for a few seconds before brushing away the teardrops that had fallen from the corners of her eyes with his thumbs as he cupped her face in his hands.

'I am going to take that a yes. Was that a nod? Excellent,' he said and he moved to kiss her again.

Only at that second the electricity came back on in a blinding brightness against the relative gloom of their cosy nest and Ella buried her face in his shirt to escape the glare.

'I think that's a sign.' Seb chuckled, and hugged Ella closer. 'You did warn me this morning that it was going to be a very *interesting* day! I can hardly wait to see what tomorrow will bring!'

* * *

Seb switched off the car engine, dropped his head back against the fine leather, and closed his eyes.

He was exhausted. Physically and mentally.

After the traumatic events of the previous day, he had found it impossible to get to sleep in the early hours of the morning and after a few hours of tossing and turning, listening to the wind howling outside the bedroom window, his mind burning hot with thoughts of Ella, he had finally admitted defeat and turned to the never-ending barrage of emails that had arrived from all over the world through a much slower connection than he was used to.

News about the PSN Media offer had still not broken but it would not take long. On Monday morning the financial papers would be looking for interviews and press statements. And, of course, he would have to tell his staff before then.

Matt had pre-recorded a simple video but that was nowhere good enough to reassure the people who worked for him. They needed details and facts. And it was his job to provide them.

So spending almost a whole day driving around the Languedoc from one Morel family to another was a luxury he could ill afford, even if his cell phone had never stopped ringing. Yet, somehow, finding out the truth about who he was and the father he had never known seemed more important than ever before.

Holding Ella in his arms last night when she told him about her past had opened a window for him on his own questions. He *could* hire a private detective and start a detailed investigation, but he knew that the Morel family would be much more likely to tell him the whole story about André Morel if they met him in person as Helene's son.

And he was right.

It had taken him several hours to put together the snatches

of thirty-year-old memories from each individual he had spoken to and create one complete picture.

But now he knew *what* had happened. And *why.* And *when.*

He could not wait to share what he had discovered with Ella.

There was no one else he *wanted* to tell.

Her trust had forged a link between them that was not going to be broken when he left for Sydney.

He slowly opened his eyes and released the tension in his shoulders.

His news could wait. *His problem. His past.*

There was one more piece of information he *could tell her*—but it could wait until tomorrow. The woman deserved one night of happiness before hard reality crept back in.

He had promised Ella Bailey an evening out and that was precisely what he was going to deliver. Time to find out if she was ready to be spoilt!

Seb strolled around the side of the house as the sun began to dip below the top of the plane trees. He could hear cicadas in the vineyard, and a nightingale on the river bank nearby. And a smooth jazz piano melody.

Ella was sitting at the piano in the living room with her eyes closed, her hands moving effortlessly across the keys. She was humming and singing along to the music that drifted out into the garden through the open patio doors, so enchanted by the song that she had not even heard his car glide up at the front of the house.

She sang in such a sweet, tender tone that he stopped, happy to simply listen to her beautiful voice.

It was such a magical sight that his senses filled with the serene beauty of the moment.

And his heart swelled to bursting just looking at her.

Ella was wearing a sleeveless blue dress the exact same colour of her eyes. Luminescent pale china-blue eyes the shade of a spring morning. It seemed to be gathered just below her breasts in the perfect place to make his blood pound and his heart beat even faster. There were flowers and beads in trailing patterns all over the short skirt that billowed out each side of the piano stool.

By Ella's standard it was positively modest and sedate.

She looked stunning.

This was the Ella who had dominated his mind every minute since he had left her that morning after spending an hour on the computer with Dan, showing him all the places where his charity projects were making a difference. Seb sucked in a breath of the sweet garden air. Somehow this amazing woman made him feel and do things that were so unexpected that they startled him.

He had never played computer games or worked on education with children before and had felt so far out of his depth it had been ridiculous—for the first ten minutes, before he had started to share the joy and excitement of a six-year-old seeing new worlds for the first time.

He was not used to acting on impulse. And he certainly wasn't used to sharing his past with people he barely knew.

But with Ella?

She made him feel that he could act differently. And that was more than unsettling.

Perhaps he was being selfish wanting to share the evening with her?

In two days he could be on a flight back to Sydney with several years of frantic project work ahead of him—and no plans to return to France.

So where did that leave him?

The implications of what he was getting into were only too clear when he thought about her little boy, whom he had become so fond of in such a short period of time. The new owner of his power torch was living in the house he grew up in, playing with the kind of dogs he used to play with. It had been such a pleasure to show Dan the wonders of the technology that was so commonplace in his own life, but seemed somehow magical to a six-year-old. The few hours he had spent with Dan had been the most fun he had experienced in a long time.

There was no way he could break Dan's heart with broken promises.

The public persona his media team had created for Sebastien Castellano was a carefully constructed myth created by experts keen to exploit the young sexy image of a man whom the cameras loved—exactly the kind of man investors wanted to know was in control of their communication systems. He could talk to TV reporters; he could walk up red carpets. But his personal life was another matter and one he never talked about.

The truth was far simpler. The truth was that he had only ever dated single girls who knew that he was not interested in a long-term relationship.

That policy had made him a very rich and successful man. And alone. There was no one waiting for him to come home to in Sydney. Or Perth or Tokyo or whatever city needed his skills. All he had waiting for him back in Sydney was an amazing high-tech apartment with every possible luxury. And emptiness.

Ella had helped him to remember how it felt to be part of a close and loving happy family.

Strange how he had been denying it to himself all of these years as he filled every second of every day with frenetic activity then went home alone to an empty apartment.

Only now? More than once that afternoon he had seriously considered driving back to Montpellier and calling Ella to say that he had to deal with a company crisis and someone would collect his bag and it would not be far from the truth. There was always some project that could use his expertise should he want to use it as an excuse. He had his passport in one pocket, his organiser in the other. He could go anywhere in the world he wanted simply by making one telephone call. He could always tell Ella that Matt needed him.

Instead he had driven back to this house. To this woman. Knowing that in his heart he wanted a few more minutes with Ella and her son when he could pretend that they were *his* family.

It would be a whole lot easier for both of them if he left now, and blamed the negotiations for dragging him away.

Walking away would be the sensible thing to do. And until now he had always been the sensible one.

Except this was Ella and Dan he was talking about. There was no way that he was prepared to lie to either of them.

And it had been worth it. Looking at Ella now, seeing her so happy, any doubts he might have had about their date or his reasons for being here were quashed.

Ella was here. Now. In this moment. That was all that mattered.

He wanted to find out if the skin on her neck and arms was as smooth as he remembered. To kiss her lips. Her stunning hair. To savour the precious time he could hold her in his arms.

He felt almost guilty looking at her when she was so caught up in the music; she was completely oblivious to anything and anyone around her.

He would have been content to stay watching her for hours except at that moment she swung her slim legs off the piano stool and raised her arms out above her head in a delicious cat stretch. And saw him. Watching her.

With one flush of embarrassment she slid her feet into

high-heeled slingback shoes and flicked her hair back over one shoulder as she stepped lightly over to the music system and pressed the play button. Classical jazz echoed out from the speakers in the living room.

'It's the other Ella Jane. Ella Jane Fitzgerald. Maybe one day I will be able to sing half as well!'

As he strolled over to join her he noticed that hanging down tantalisingly between her breasts was a necklace made up of an odd assortment of objects. Shells, beads, precious stones set in silver, a collection as unique as she was. It suited her perfectly.

Then something sparkled and he focused again, while trying not to ogle at her bosom.

A thin circle of gold inset with diamonds and sapphires hung from one of the loops of her necklace. A quick glance at her ring finger confirmed it.

She had taken off her wedding ring.

Something inside him suddenly felt light and in the mood to join in the singing, preferably something with hallelujah in it.

'I like your necklace,' he said, trying to sound calm and casual.

Her lips pressed together for a fraction of a second in recognition and understanding. 'Thank you, it's new.' Only then she tilted her head to one side like a curious bird as she moved her shoulders from side to side in tune with the music. 'You look very pleased with yourself. Are you going to tell me where you went today? You do know that I will wangle it out of you eventually, don't you?'

The joyous, playful tone of her voice was so contagious that Seb could not contain a tiny bubble of happiness, which emerged as a chuckle. And then another.

'That's for later. And where is the man of the house?' he

asked, pretending to look over her shoulder into the garden and then the house. 'I come with date gifts.'

'Gifts? A box of lovely chocolates would be nice. Or perhaps a new fairy godmother to provide some glass slippers?'

Seb snorted. 'Please! As if I was that predictable?' He swung a large heavy plastic bag from an upmarket electrical store onto the patio table. 'The store didn't do gift wrapping. I hope Dan likes it.'

Ella peeked inside, looked at Seb with a puzzled expression, then pulled out two large cartons from inside the bag.

'How *very* thoughtful of you, but, er, what are webcams?'

Seb shook his head. 'Dan told me that he was going to visit his grandparents next week, and I thought you mind find these useful. Think of it as a video camera attached to your computer. If you both have webcams, you can see each other and talk live. Every day if you like. Perhaps I had better set it up for you in the morning?'

'I think you had better,' Ella replied as she read the information on the side of the box. 'Wow. I can see and talk to Dan through the computer any time I like? Well. That is, without doubt, the nicest date present I have ever received. Thank you; they are just what I have always wanted. Wait until I tell Dan! He already thinks that you are totally cool!'

'I aim to please.' Seb laughed and pulled out a wrist corsage with a single fresh pale orchid blossom from inside his jacket pocket. 'I know. I am hopelessly old-fashioned. But I hope you like it. Sorry it's a bit crushed.'

Ella sucked in a breath and held her whole body still for a moment as she stared at the orchid as though it were an object from a distant planet.

Seb's face fell. 'You hate it.'

'Oh, no, nothing like that,' Ella replied with a smile, trying to quickly reassure him. 'It's just that it has been a long time since a man bought me flowers. I didn't realise until right now just how much I missed that. Thank you. I love it.'

She quickly popped the flower onto her wrist and held out her arm to admire it.

'Perfect.'

'Um. I would have to agree,' Seb replied, only his gaze hadn't left Ella's face. 'Is Dan here?'

'Oh, young mister Daniel is currently enjoying the delightful company of his school friends at a party at Sandrine's. Apparently there are two birthdays to celebrate next week.'

She grinned. 'Yvette will be bringing him home later and either playing with Dan or trying to get him to bed, depending on the amount of sugar and artificial colourings he has stuffed himself with. I suspect industrial quantities of ice cream and cake will be involved so he will probably still be bouncing when we get back.' Then she added,' I did warn her that it could be a little late.'

'Wise move.' Seb nodded. 'I understand that these musical soirées can sometimes go on after ten in the evening,' he added in a mock serious tone. 'How shocking!'

He looked behind him from side to side, then whispered, 'And there might even be dancing, but please don't tell anyone I said that.'

'Of course not.' Ella frowned. 'Actually I am not one for dancing. I know it's weird.' She shrugged. 'I adore the music but the feet don't move where they should do.'

She stuck out her legs and twirled her ankles. 'I think it comes from being left-handed. I move left and everyone else moves right. Which is the other left, if you know what I mean, which I know you don't? Then my face goes as red as my partner's toes.'

She shook her head. 'I'll be quite happy just dancing along by myself. Disco style. Much safer for all concerned.'

Seb snorted in disbelief. 'Disco! You are the most musical

person I have ever met, so your pitiful excuses do not work on me.' And he strolled up to her and extended both hands palm upwards. 'May I have the honour of this dance, *mademoiselle*?'

CHAPTER TEN

ELLA bathed in the heat of Seb's gaze as he smiled down at her, clearly determined to make her dance. He looked sexier and even more handsome and any resolve *she* might have had to stay on her piano stool seemed to melt like ice.

In seconds they were on the patio under the moonlight.

Her senses were so alive when he was close like this. The garden suddenly seemed full of the sound of birdsong and insects. Bees from the honeysuckle, thyme and lavender were the soundtrack to the beat of her heart and the soft music playing in the house. It was magical. Tonight they sang for her. And for Sebastien. And only for them.

She simply could not resist him. And it had absolutely nothing to do with the fact that he looked every inch the same multimillionaire businessman whose photos she had been polishing for months. No. It was the man under the suit.

Oops. She had a vision of Seb minus his clothes. Big oops.

Ella willed down the intense blush she could feel on her cheeks as she felt Seb clasp hold of her fingers and draw her to him.

'Thank you, sir. How kind of you to think of us poor wallflowers. All alone and overlooked.'

'Um. Right. You have never been a wallflower in your life, Miss Bailey. You look amazing. That dress…' He exaggerated a shiver then hissed, 'Amazing,' making Ella's blush even hotter. And with one swift tug on her hands she was in his arms. One hand slid strategically onto her waist, the other clasped firmly around her palm. And her body…her body pressed tightly against his chest.

'Exactly what kind of dance is this?' she dared to ask, her nose about two inches away from the open neck of Seb's shirt, so that she could see the dark hairs on his chest below the St Christopher pendant. He smelt of expensive cologne and something musky, spicy and arousing—something that was uniquely Sebastien. A flash of something horribly close to desire ran through her body, startling her with its intensity.

Her back straightened and her head lifted away as she tried to regain her self-control, only to become suddenly aware that the music compilation she had selected for Nicole's party had changed to a lively upbeat rhythm of a South American tango.

Instantly Seb drew her even closer, so that his hips moved against hers, swaying from side to side. Taking her with him. She had no choice but to follow his actions, his broad chest and strong legs pressed so close to the thin fabric of her silk dress that she felt glued to him along the whole length of his body.

'Latin, of course,' he replied, his voice close to her ear and muffled by her hair. Rough, urgent. She was clearly not the only one who was starting to become rather warm. 'Lots of shuffling and stamping. Leg twisting and dipping comes later…although.'

He stopped talking and Ella took a deep breath and asked 'Although?'

His hand moved sinuously up her back as the pace increased and his legs started moving faster. 'Perhaps not in that dress. It is…' and he sighed, the implications only too obvious as his fingers splayed on the bare skin of her back and his grip tightened '…far, far too tempting.' And without warning he leant forward from the waist, so that she moved backwards chest to chest, both of his hands taking her weight with effortless ease and agility. Except that she had been so captivated by his words that she had not seen the move coming and her arms clenched hard around his neck to stop herself from falling backwards and she cried out in alarm.

With a gentle movement Seb slowly brought her back to a standing position, his hands drawing her closer and holding her against him as she dragged in ragged breaths of air in a feeble attempt to calm her heart rate.

'Sorry,' she eventually managed to squeak out, feeling like a complete idiot. She knew that Seb would never let her fall. She had overreacted, her body once more letting her down.

Seb paused and released her long enough so that they could look into each other's eyes as his fingers spread wide so that they could caress her skin in delicious soft circles.

His forehead pressed against hers so that his voice reverberated through her skull. Hot, concerned, tender and understanding.

'You have to trust me and let me lead, Ella. Can you try?'

Ella closed her eyes and tried to calm her heartbeat and failed. Her mind was spinning as his words hit home, all the while Seb's body was pressed close to her, filling her senses with his masculine scent and the sheer physicality of him.

She knew that he was talking about more than placing her faith in a dance partner. And part of her shrank back from the edge.

She had never truly allowed anyone to lead her. Not deep down. In fact the more she thought about it, the more she knew that she had always danced to her own beat.

His breath was hot on her face as he patiently waited for the answer that would decide where they went from here. And not just for the evening. He was asking her to trust him with nothing less than her heart. Was he also asking her to trust him with her future and her dreams?

'I…don't know,' she whispered, her heart thumping so hard that she was sure that he must be able to hear it, but not daring to open her eyes. It would be too much.

'Then perhaps I can persuade you?'

Gentle pressure lifted her chin and, although her eyes were still clamped tight shut, she felt every tiny movement of his body as his nose pressed against her cheek, his breath hot and fast in time with the heart beating against her dress.

A soft mouth nuzzled against her upper lip and she sighed in pleasure as one of his hands slid back to caress the base of her head, holding her firm against him.

The stubble on his chin and neck rasped against her skin as he pressed gentle kisses down her temple to the hollow below her ear. Each kiss drove her wild with the delicious languorous sensation of skin on skin.

He was totally intoxicating.

The tenderness and exquisite delicacy of each kiss was more than she could have imagined possible from Seb. More caring. More loving… Loving. Yes. They were the kisses of a lover. *Her* lover. And it felt so very right.

Which was why she did something she had believed until a few short days ago would never happen again. She brought her arms even tighter around Seb's neck and notched her head up towards him.

And with eyes still closed, Ella kissed him on the mouth.

His hands stilled for a moment and she paused to suck in a terrified breath, trembling that she had made the most almighty mistake. Until now *he* had kissed her. This would change everything. What if she totally misunderstood what he had told her? And he only wanted to lead? Not share.

She felt him shift beneath her, and, daring to open her eyes, she stared into a smile as wide as it was welcome, but then his mouth pressed hotter and deeper onto hers, blowing away any hint of doubt that he wanted her just as much as she needed him with the depth of his passion and delight.

A shuddering sigh of relief ran through her and she grinned back in return and buried her face deep into the corner of his neck. His hands ran up and down her back, thrilling her with the heat of their touch as his lips kissed her brow and her hair.

Kisses so natural and tender it felt as though she had been waiting for them all of her life.

Every sensation seemed heightened. The warmth of the fading sun on her arms, the touch of his fingertips on her skin, the softness of his shirt under her cheek and the fast beat of his heart below the fine fabric.

It was Seb who broke the silence. 'Now will you trust me?' He was trying to keep his voice light and playful but she knew him too well now, and revelled in the fact that she was the source of his hoarse, low whisper, intense with something more fundamental and earthy.

The fingers of one of his hands were playing with her hair, but she could feel his heartbeat slow just a little when she chuckled into his shirt, then turned his face towards the sun.

'Well, I just might. We are talking about dancing. Aren't we?'

His warm laughter filled her heart to bursting.

'Of course. Although I do have one request. I have an appointment with a very special lady who I haven't visited for eighteen years. And I'd like you to come and meet her. Do you mind if we stop in on the way?'

* * *

Sebastien Castellano stood in silence at the foot of the grave in the tiny village cemetery and gently lowered the bouquet of his mother's favourite white roses from the Mas Tournesol onto the engraved granite monument.

Stepping back, he wrapped one arm around Ella's waist, then slowly read out the words chiselled into the hard stone surface out loud.

'Helene Laurence Castellano. Beloved daughter, wife and mother.'

He closed his eyes for a second and thought about the portrait hanging in the living room back at the house that had been their home. And the lovely woman smiling back at him, captured for ever in a moment in time.

Nothing to indicate the devastation her death had brought to all of her family.

His father had suffered six months of agony before packing their bags and putting them as many miles as he could from this peaceful, beautiful Languedoc village where Helene had made her home.

Even if that meant dragging his angry and confused twelve-year-old son with him all the way to Australia. He would probably have chosen a remote island in the Pacific if the international bank he worked for had been able to transfer him there!

'My father chose the inscription. He said that there were not enough words to describe the wonderful person my mother had been. And he was right. How do you put into a few lines the joy and laughter and energy of such an amazing, smart, pretty, funny and creative woman I was lucky enough to know as my mother? It's impossible. All you can do is remember her how she was and hold that memory every day of your life.'

'Oh, Seb. I am so sorry.'

Sebastien sighed as Ella wrapped her arms as far around his waist as she could, and leant her head on his jacket.

'How did it happen?' she asked quietly after a long drawn out silence.

'Brain tumour. I remember coming home from school a few times and she was lying down with a headache. She blamed it on too much sun and rosé wine with lunch.' Seb lifted his head and swallowed down the lump of pain that had built up. 'She never complained. Then one Saturday morning my father came in from the garden and found her lying on the kitchen floor having some sort of seizure.'

Seb looked up into the poplar trees. 'I remember that day so clearly. I was helping out at my grandmother's and we were all meeting up for lunch. It was a lovely spring day, birds were singing and we had been laughing and messing about. Just having fun. Only when we got to the Mas the ambulance was outside.'

He did not dare look at her. 'They thought it was a stroke at first. She could still talk and get around and keep up the pretence that everything was okay, but later the seizures got worse. In the end there was nothing the hospital doctors could do to help her. She asked us to take her home so that she could spend her last days in the one place she loved more than anything.'

Ella sucked in a breath. 'The Mas. Did she…?'

The words were left unsaid but Seb simply nodded. 'We set up a bedroom in the room next to the kitchen where the living room is now. Eighteen years ago, today, my dad and I sat with her for the last time. She was looking out of the window and smiling at the roses—these white roses—so I ran out and snipped off a blossom to give to her, and when I got back inside…she was gone. Oh, Mum, I am so sorry. So very, very sorry.'

Tears were running down his cheeks now, and Ella turned around and gathered him to her, holding him tight until his head fell onto her shoulder and his body relaxed enough for his arms to embrace her. The taut muscles in his chest quivered with such deep emotion that her own eyes filled with tears.

His mother had passed away in the house where she cleaned and cooked and was bringing up her son. How could he *not* feel conflicted? And Nicole was his stepmother. Who used the Mas Tournesol as her holiday home. As somewhere she could hold parties in the summer.

Ella winced. *Oh, no.* The realisation hit her so hard that she lifted her arms and reached around Seb's neck, her fingers caressing his head. Nicole was holding her birthday party only a few days after the anniversary of Seb's mum's death.

Oh, Nicole. Do you even know how important this date is to Seb?

She stood on tiptoe to press her lips against his full mouth, and then his cheek, and his arms tightened into a warm hug, as though he needed to wrap himself in her understanding and sympathy.

If only it could be enough!

'I found out who André Morel is today. It turns out that I was right after all. He did let her down, only not in the way I had imagined.'

'Oh, Seb,' she replied, taking his hand in hers.

'André was nineteen when he asked my mother to marry him. Apparently a few weeks before the wedding he told his parents that he couldn't go through with it. He wasn't ready to settle down and be a husband and work in the bank like his own father had done.'

Seb turned slightly and braved a small proud smile. 'And my mother let him go. She didn't want him to feel trapped and she loved him enough to let him leave her and set off around the world without her.'

'She must have been a remarkable woman,' Ella whispered. 'And what about Luc Castellano? How did she meet him?'

'Luc was André's boss and a good friend to both of them. He was going to be the best man at their wedding. The Morel family suspected that he was in love with her. What they didn't know was that he loved her enough to offer her marriage when she found out she was pregnant. Do you know the strangest thing? As far as his family are concerned, it was a teenage romance and my mother fell into the arms of her friend Luc Castellano to console herself on the rebound. She never told André about me.'

'So he never knew he had a son. What are you going to do?'

He stared at her hand, fascinated by the pattern her fingers and his made as they meshed and twisted and turned. 'I could make the calls. Find an address for André and his new family in Canada. But I won't. I already have a father. And it turns out that he is a damn good one. One of these days I might even tell him that to his face.'

'Oh, Seb. He loved you, even though you were someone else's son. And he still does.'

Her fingers moved below the hair on his neck and closed around the links of a fine chain. Sensing the pressure, Seb released his bear grip and stood back a little to lift one arm and released the St Christopher that was hidden beneath his business shirt.

Ella fingered the small oval medallion hanging from the chain in silence, waiting for him to speak.

'The last time I stood in this spot was with my maternal grandmother. She hung it around my neck and told me that it would keep me safe on my travels until I was ready to come home. I've worn it every day since. I suppose it is a little old-fashioned but it means a lot.'

Seb looked down at Ella and smiled a crooked, lopsided smile. 'The women in my life have a very annoying habit of being right. I suppose I had better get used to that.'

Ella's heart skipped a beat. 'What are you saying, Seb? Am I part of your life?'

His smile widened and he turned away slightly so that he could grasp hold of her hand. Ella sighed in silent contentment as they stood side by side looking out across the stunningly pretty cemetery, past the poplars and yew trees to the rows of sunflowers and vines that stretched out to the low green hills beyond the village in the fading light.

'I haven't been here for eighteen years. And I chose you to share this moment with you. Does that answer your question, Ella?'

Ella smiled and looked down at the roses, their petals fluttering in the warm breeze, and hot tears pricked the corners of her eyes as her throat closed. Seb's fingers meshed between hers, giving her strength as she fought the intensity of the feelings that bound them together. Her only answer was a sharp nod and a whispered, 'Yes. Yes, it does.'

He kissed the top of her head and turned back to face her, then lifted her knuckles to his lips. 'I'll turn the car around. See you in a minute.' And with one small kiss on her forehead he released her hand and strolled back down the grass towards the narrow lane leading up to the church, leaving her bereft. 'Be right there,' she said under her breath, overcome with a riot of sadness and tenderness and devotion and something she had known only once in her life. Something she imagined that she had lost for ever.

She was falling in love with Sebastien Castellano.

Which was just about the craziest thing she had ever done—crazy even by her definition of normal. In a few days Nicole and her sixtieth birthday party would be a happy memory, Dan would be in Spain with his grandparents and Seb would be thousands of miles away in, well, in whatever country he was working in at that moment. Whether it was

Sydney or Seattle one thing was certain. It would not be here, in the village where he grew up.

Ella rearranged the flowers on the granite and smiled down at the monument to a woman who had loved her son as much as she loved her own little boy.

Perhaps his grandmother had only been partly right. Yes, Seb had come home, but perhaps he had only come home for a visit. Not to stay. Not to rebuild a life for himself. Just passing through.

Like a tornado leaving destruction in his wake.

Which made going out on a date with him this evening an even crazier decision!

'Yvette? Are you still awake?' Ella whispered, peering into the living room, frightened of waking Dan, as she yawned widely. She had dozed off for a few minutes in the warmth of the car with her new smooth jazz CD playing on the impressive car music system. And Seb sitting next to her chatting happily away.

Still smiling languorously at the memory of one of the most amazing musical evenings of her life, Ella grinned as Yvette rustled in from the kitchen, very much awake and dressed in her outdoor clothing.

'Ella? Is that you? Have you seen Dan?'

'Dan?' Ella repeated, suddenly alert. There was something in the tone of Yvette's voice that sent a cold shiver down her spine, but she shrugged it off. A windy night with his mother away was bound to unsettle him. 'Is he still up watching cartoons? Not to worry, I'll soon get him settled.'

'Dan isn't watching cartoons, Ella. He's not in his bed. I think he's gone out looking for that stupid old dog.' Yvette reached out and grabbed Ella's arm. 'I am so sorry. This is my entire fault.'

At two a.m. Ella might not have been at her best, but the

words seared into her brain like a shower of icy water. Not in his bed?

She grabbed her friend around both shoulders, forcing her to make eye contact, even though they were both shaking.

'When was the last time you saw him? Please,' Ella managed to get out through a closed throat.

'I checked him about one. He was fast asleep!'

Her head dropped onto her chest. 'I settled down to read the paper,' and her voice came now as a trembling rush, 'and like the old fool that I am I must have dozed off long enough for the boy to slip past me.' Yvette looked up at Ella with tears in her eyes. 'I am so sorry.'

Ella ran upstairs and flicked on the light in Dan's bedroom. The nightlight was still on. The wardrobe doors were open. His boots and jacket were missing. So was the new power torch that Seb had given him.

Suddenly aware that she was wearing thin sandals, Ella fled back to the hall, shrugged on a waterproof jacket and her gardening clogs, flung open the front door against the strong wind, and ran into Seb's arms.

He held her trembling body against his before lifting her fearful face in both hands for a second and asking in a voice so loving and caring that she almost lost it, 'Hey! What's going on?'

'It's Dan. He's gone missing.'

CHAPTER ELEVEN

Dan! Seb's heart contracted and he took a moment to calm his breathing.

If anything happened to that little boy he did not know what he would do! If this was what being a full-time parent was like, it was terrifying!

Seb held Ella against his side, the trembling of her fragile body forcing him to make decisions before she started to panic. 'He won't have gone very far. Not in the dark.'

He turned back to Yvette, who had started to sob.

Oh, no. Time to take charge and use the quick brain and problem-solving skills he was famous for, even if he did feel like floundering.

'Yvette. I know this is hard, but please try to remember,' he said in a quiet calm voice in the local dialect, trying to quell his own anxiety as much as Ella's. 'Did Dan give you any clue that he was going outside?'

'He told me that Milou was still inside the barn, and the wind was howling and he was frightened that he would not be able to get to sleep without his dog. I told him that Milou would be okay and he could see him in the morning. He seemed to accept that…' Her voice trailed off.

Seb kissed the top of Ella's head so that his words were muffled by her hair but still sounded clear and echoing across the silence of the hallway. 'The barn? That's as good a place as any to start. Did he take the new torch?'

His arm slipped from around Ella's waist as she answered with a quick nod, and she almost snatched at it, the loss was so great. 'Ella, you are with me,' he replied, bustling them both into the kitchen and passing Ella the small torch. 'Yvette. Why don't you make a start on the hot chocolate? We'll be back as fast as we can.'

Seb turned back to face Ella and he took a firm hold of both of her forearms, demanding her attention so that when her eyes locked onto his Seb's words were focused on her and her alone.

'We're going to need more light. You make a head start towards the barn, and I'll bring the car around and catch up as soon as I can,' and with one hot, hard kiss on her lips he was out of the door and into the night.

'I like him,' Yvette whispered through a choked throat. 'Helene would have been proud of her boy.'

'I like him too,' Ella sniffed, 'but I don't know what I'm going to do about that.'

'You'll think of something. Now get out there and find Dan. Those torch batteries won't last all night and he could get scared.'

The rumble of a powerful car engine reverberated around the silent kitchen. The beautiful shiny red sports car edged its way onto the patio across the grass like a cruise ship coming into harbour. Only this ship was knocking over the stone flower urns as it went, destroying the bodywork in the process.

Ella ran out into the garden as Seb swung the car around so that the powerful headlights illuminated the top part of the barn doors, which were closed tight shut. She tugged hard at the latch but it refused to move, and Ella's chest heaved with tears of frustration as she struggled against the wind and the heavy wooden latch, terrified about what she might find inside and furious that she could not reach Dan.

'The wind has blown the barn doors tight shut,' Seb called, jogging behind Ella so that they tugged at the heavy latch on the door at the same time. The door flew backwards in the force of the gusting wind and they both lunged inside.

Looking back at them from the seat of an old stuffed chair was a little boy with his arm around his dog sitting warm and cosy under Ella's old quilt and reading his cartoon book by torchlight. A bottle of juice and an empty biscuit packet lay at his feet.

'Hello, Mummy. We're having a midnight picnic. Seb's torch is so cool. Will you read me a story?'

Ella leant against her kitchen table and closed her tired eyes. So much had happened since she had left Dan with Yvette that it felt as though *days* had passed rather than merely a few hours. A few *precious* hours when she had been able to spend time alone with Sebastien on a simple dinner date and concert.

Only nothing was simple where Sebastien was concerned.

Deep pain cramped around her heart when she thought about what could have happened to Dan when he was out alone in the night.

Part of her was proud that her little boy was strong and brave enough to go out in the dark in a storm to find his old dog, but the cold, gut-wrenching fear of that moment when she found his bed empty overwhelmed her once again, and Ella collapsed down onto the kitchen chair and wrapped her arms around her raised knees, not caring that it would cause serious creases in her best party frock.

She had only been gone for a few hours! And look what had happened!

Tears streamed down her face, ruining the clever make-up she had taken an hour to perfect so that she could look great on her first date in years.

The emotions of the evening were finally starting to take their toll and she now knew what being twisted around inside a tornado must be like.

The wonderful, magical evening she had spent with Seb had been turned on its head, and now? Now she barely knew her own name.

One thing, however, was crystal clear. She was never going to be selfish and put her own needs ahead of Dan again.

It had been *her* decision to stay out and enjoy herself a lot longer than she had planned, and Yvette had encouraged her to do so, but the impact of that decision had consequences.

Dan needed her to take care of him. She was the only family he had. His two sets of grandparents were either travelling on tour in some remote part of the world where health care was a distant dream, or holed up inside their luxurious town house in Barcelona, trapped inside walls of loss and grief.

No. Dan was her responsibility. And tonight…tonight she had failed him.

For a few hours she had been given a glimpse of her old life and she had loved it. And now she was paying the price. Her instincts had been right. She could not combine the role of single mother with life as a performer. It simply did not work.

There was a shuffle in the doorway and her traitorous heart skipped a beat in both pleasure and guilt as Sebastien stepped into the kitchen and drew her up out of the chair and into the warmth of his embrace.

'Dan is fast asleep. That little man has had a big day. And so has his mum.'

Ella looked into Seb's lovely eyes and tried to smile through a trembling jaw.

He instantly seemed to pick up on her distress and wrapped his arms around her back, pressing her head into the warmth of his chest, his love and devotion only too clear.

Ella blinked away tears of happiness as he dropped a kiss on the top of her head and rubbed the small of her back.

'I know you were scared. But he is fine. Just fine.'

Her voice trembled with delight at his touch. 'I know, it's not Dan. It's me. I was the one who was terrified this time.'

Seb held her tighter for a second and then his arms relaxed and he guided her gently back into a chair.

He sat down opposite her and stared into her eyes as he brushed a strand of hair back behind her ear with his fingertips, the delicious sensation so hypnotic and so welcoming that she felt like sighing in delight.

'You can't blame yourself,' Seb said in a low voice. 'You did everything you could to keep him safe. But you have one very determined little boy.'

He reached across the table and took one of her hands in his, caressing her palm with his thumb.

'I've just talked to him man to man about sneaking out late at night on his own without telling anyone where he was going and scaring the living daylights out of his mum and his babysitter. He won't be doing that again.'

His wry smile melted her resolve and she managed a gentle grin as she pushed her shoulders back with a shudder.

'Thank you for that. And for helping me to look for him. I just keep thinking that I should have seen it coming. He knows that his grandparents love him, but being away from home for two long weeks is a big deal when you are six years old.'

'How about when you are twenty-eight?' He paused for a second, then took both of her hands in his, and focused completely on her face, forcing her to give him her total attention.

'I spoke to Nicole this afternoon. The flights are booked out so you should expect her Tuesday. And she did tell me something else. Something important. Nicole is thinking of selling this house so that she can start a new life for herself. And it could mean a new fresh start for you and Dan at the same time, Ella.'

Blood surged to her brain, making her dizzy and light-headed. Her mind tried to cope with the meaning of the words while fighting to reject them at the same time and started spinning downwards in a spiral of terror.

'Nicole can't be selling the house. She told me that she loved it here!'

Ella's head reeled with the implications and she slid her fingers from Seb's and pushed herself onto her feet, using the edge of the table to steady herself as she shook her head and stared at Seb in disbelief.

'Wait a moment. Did you just say that you spoke to Nicole this afternoon? You knew! You knew what she was planning and you never said a word all evening! How could you do that, Seb? How could you not tell me that I was about to lose my home?'

'Because I didn't want anything to spoil our evening together. You have so little time for yourself, Ella. You deserved a few hours away from reality.'

She clasped tighter onto the hard, well-worn wood, her knuckles white with the pressure. She wanted to be happy for Nicole but every part of her screamed out at her own loss.

'You don't understand. This house is not just my job. I love it here.'

Glancing frantically around the room, Ella raised one hand towards the watercolours she had painted of the garden and Dan's artwork on the refrigerator. 'This is the only home Dan and I have ever truly known. These walls are my rock. I need this, Seb. I need this house. And so does Dan.'

She closed her eyes and a glimmer of hope flicked through her brain. 'Perhaps the new owner needs a housekeeper. Nicole can give me a good recommendation. That's a possibility, isn't it?'

There was so much doubt and fear in her voice that Seb walked swiftly around the table and gathered her into his arms, soothing her with calming words before pressing his forehead gently against her brow so that he could smile into her tear-filled eyes.

'There is another option. I know this has come out of the blue for both of us but there is another option. I want you to come away with me. You and Dan. We can make it work, Ella. I know we can.'

His words stunned her with a sense of such wonder and delight that she took a step back and battled to sort through the confusion of thrill, excitement and terror.

'What do you mean…come to Montpellier with you tomorrow, or come to Sydney with you?'

'Sydney, of course,' he replied, raising both hands in the air and glancing around the kitchen. 'I realise that my penthouse won't be quite as exciting as a farmhouse without electricity or midnight picnics in a storm,' he added, grinning, 'but I think you would love it. Being with you and Dan these last few days has shown me what I have been missing in my life. We can be a family, Ella.'

The excitement and enthusiasm in his voice beamed out in the kitchen, filling it with energy and power and vitality. His hands moved to stroke her face and his smile bored deep into the core of her soul with such love and fierce passion that it broke her heart, but that did not make it any easier to slip out of his arms and step across to the open kitchen door.

She needed to clear her head. And fast.

Seb followed her and she wallowed in the wonderful sensation of his arms wrapped around her waist as he laid his head on her shoulder so they both looked out onto the moonlit garden where they had danced together only a few hours earlier.

'Come to Australia with me. And be my love.'

She breathed in the heavy scent of him mingled with the night-flowering nicotiana, the musk roses around the door and what remained of her precious perfume. His words were liquid honey on her frayed nerves, soothing and so welcoming and warm that she allowed her senses to revel in them.

There was no sound. The fierce winds had died down to a breeze and as they stood there, clasped together, a nightingale sang out from the plane trees that bordered the river, filling the night air with its wonderful song.

Calling her with music and joy because it was singing its own true song.

Her heart broke because now she knew that she had the strength to say what she wanted for herself and Dan.

She forced herself to turn inside the curve of his arms and took hold of his face with both of her hands and held it steady, so that she could force out the words that she needed to say before her courage failed her.

'I am happy for you, Seb. I truly am. You deserve every success and I know that you are going to do wonderful work with your charity. But I can't come with you to Sydney. My home is here. In this small village in the Languedoc. Not in the city.'

His handsome face twisted in confusion and he replied in a voice crackling with hesitancy.

'I know this has come fast and it's a lot to take in, but you know that you and Dan will never want for anything. Dan will get the best education and his wonderful, amazing mother can have her choice of singing coaches and start performing again anywhere she likes. In a few years you could rebuild your career. It would be great.'

Ella smiled through her tears in understanding. 'I know that you mean well. You can offer us the best that money can buy. But there are other things we need which will be harder to find in the city.'

She paused as the impact of what she was saying hit hard, and deep crease lines appeared on his brow as he shook his head.

'What do you mean? What other things?'

She bit her lip. Seb had created an ideal picture for their life together in the city, which was brilliant, and yet it all seemed suddenly too much to take in all at once. She had already been through this situation when Christobal's parents had planned her life in Barcelona without consulting her. They had acted out of love, she understood that now, but trying to fit into another person's lifestyle and rules in a modern city had almost destroyed her.

'Peace. Tranquillity. Calm. A garden where I can pick fruit from the trees. Somewhere for Dan to play and run around all day. A community where he feels safe and welcome and his grandparents are within driving distance. And his dog, of course. And something else. Something even more important than any of those things.'

Ella looked hard at him. Could she take that risk in another city with Seb? And what would that do to Dan? He adored Seb. But was Seb ready to be a father to her little boy?

'Can you give us yourself, Seb? Your time and your love and your heart? Not money or possessions. Dan needs people, not possessions. I need you. Can you put us ahead of anything else in your life? Because otherwise I will be repeating exactly the same mistake that Luc Castellano made after your mother died.'

His lips came together and the dark eyebrows twisted more fiercely but he allowed her to continue without interrupting.

'How did you feel when you were wrenched thousands of miles away from this house and your life without having any say in the matter? Don't you see? I would be doing exactly the same thing to Dan as your father did to you. And that is just not fair to Dan.'

Seb inhaled a deep breath and tilted his head, but his smile had faded.

'So you want to stay here and settle for a life without passion in it? Is that right? Have I understood correctly?'

'Of course I would love to travel and work but this has to be my decision!'

He shook his head. 'You're forgetting something. I may only have met you a few days ago but I know you, Ella Bailey. I know the girl who played the piano at Sandrine's the other night. I saw the way you loved the music more than the people around you. You were born with a passion for music and performing. Not settling for some comfortable life. Don't you see? You have made this house and this life a nice safe cage. A fantasy life complete with a child and a pretend family of friends and neighbours.'

She tried to move away but he held her firmly in his arms before going on.

'You can try and deny it as much as you like, but you are the one who asked for the truth. Remember? Well, I'll give you the truth.'

He reached forwards and lifted up her charm necklace with one finger.

'As far as I can tell you have used that wedding ring and your child as a barrier to any form of relationship with any other man after Christobal. That wedding ring screams out, *"Look at me, the poor single mother, and the poor young widow!"* Well, I've seen through that charade, Ella, and I'm telling you that you have just as much passion inside of you as you ever had!'

His voice softened.

'You can do anything you want. If you want to stay as a cocktail pianist, watching other people having fun from your place in the background, then fine! Do it! But if you want to take back the life you deserve for yourself and find the kind of happiness where you are the one out front on the stage—then you are going to have to learn to trust yourself.'

'What do you mean?' she asked hesitantly. 'Trust myself?'

'I watched you tonight at the jazz concert. Chatting to the other musicians and improvising on the piano just for fun. You have such a wonderful talent, Ella. Even I can see that. You were meant to be out there on a stage! Singing! Playing! Living the music—and trusting yourself to be wonderful. Because you are wonderful. You are beautiful. Talented. A joy. And the world should have a chance to see that for themselves.'

'You think I'm good?'

'I think you're better than good.'

He smiled and flicked his finger under her nose. 'And now you are fishing for compliments. I take that as a good sign.'

Seb's arms wrapped around her, snuggling her closer, his hands running up and down her back, his long fingers finding every sensitive spot.

'Will you do it? Will you take the risk? All I want is a chance to prove how much you mean to me.'

Her head lifted long enough for him to smile back at her before collapsing down against Seb's shoulder.

'I am scared. It has been such a long time.'

'I know you are. And not just about performing in public.'

He played with a strand of her hair as his cheek moved against her head.

'Sorry I raised my voice. Strange how my bad temper only surfaces when it comes to people I care about. I do care, Ella. I care very deeply. And, yes, I heard what you said. Would moving to Sydney with me be so very terrible? I'll buy us a real house with a garden where Dan can have as many dogs as he wants, right next to the beach. I have a great life there and it would be wonderful to share it with the two of you.'

'This is all too much, too fast. And it has been quite a day!'

'You don't have to make a decision now. But will you think about it? I have to go to a meeting tomorrow but I'm coming back to see Nicole. Can we talk again in a few days? Yes? Then goodnight, sweetheart. Goodnight.'

He tilted her head and kissed her with all of the love and devotion he could bring, a kiss from the heart. Because he was leaving her with his heart and his future in her hands.

Ella closed down the lid on Dan's suitcase and pressed the palm of her hand flat against the cartoon characters. She had never been apart from Dan except for occasional sleepovers at the homes of school friends and now, of all times, when she needed to be with him so badly, she knew that it was time to let him go.

Time to put the past behind her.

Time to make peace with Christobal's parents.

Of course, they were still in pain and always would be. They had lost their only son.

Ella's heart flinched at the very idea of losing her little boy. It was too horrible to even imagine. Christobal lived on through Dan and he should spend time with his grand-parents and through them come to know more about his father. The very human, talented young man she had fallen in love with.

Seb was right.

The Martinez family treasured and loved Dan and she knew that he could not be in safer or more loving care. She was the one who had to learn to accept that the only thing they had ever been concerned about was Dan's welfare. And she totally respected that.

All she had to do was trust them to believe in her. By showing them that she was the best and only mother that Dan could want.

Milou barked a rough call to Wolfie in the garden below Dan's window, and she looked out onto the sunlit flower beds that made up the safe, small world she had created for herself and Dan.

Was she a coward? Too terrified to leave the nest for fear of falling to the ground?

Perhaps she was. And all of the security she had worked so hard to build was simply an illusion to be blown away in the sea breeze.

In a few days Nicole would be back to celebrate her birthday—and Seb had promised to stay in France until she returned. Then she would have to face Seb and give him her answer.

Could she do it? Could she pretend that she was not thinking about him every waking second? Caring about him? Wondering what he was doing and where he was at that moment?

Because once he had made his peace with Nicole, then there would be nothing to keep him in this small French village full of painful memories.

The sound of barking echoed up the staircase and she smiled, inhaled deeply, slung an overstuffed bag over one shoulder and grabbed the small suitcase.

Dealing with the fallout from Seb was one thing, but keeping it together and helping Dan was something else altogether. Especially when they were about to spend several hours on a train taking him away from this house, which had been the only home he had ever known.

Ella deposited the luggage in the hall and strolled casually through the kitchen and leant against the doorpost, arms crossed. Dan was sitting with his back against the stone table, hardly looking at Milou and Wolfie, who were playing happily in the early morning sunshine. They were completely adorable and she knew that at any other time he would be out there rolling in the grass with them.

Dan had something in his hands that she could not make out, but as she walked casually over to him and kissed the top of his head Dan turned his face up towards her and his loss was marked so clearly that it almost broke her.

He misses Seb. *So do I.*

The question that had haunted her dreams played now like a record stuck on repeat. Perhaps she should have accepted Seb's offer immediately? For Dan's sake if not for hers? Perhaps they could have found a way to be happy in Sydney?

No. She had tried that in Barcelona and it had crushed her spirits. She had to be sure.

'Hey, sweetie. Ready to go and see Grandma and Grandpa in Spain? Aunty Sandrine's car will be here soon to take us to the station and we don't want to miss the train!'

Dan sniffed and his lower lip quivered.

Oh, no, don't do that! Please. Or we will both start weeping.

'Don't want to go. Want to stay here.'

Okay. She dropped down and sat next to Dan on the stone patio so that when he snuggled next to her she could wrap one arm around his shoulders and hold him tight.

Being man of the house was tough for a six-year-old.

'You know that Seb had to go to work. But what have you got there?' she asked as Dan looked down at the fine chain wrapped around his fingers. The metal glinted in the sunshine. Seb's St Christopher! The one he had shown her at the cemetery.

Ella closed her eyes and swallowed down the tears that had been threatening to force their way to the surface from the moment the tail lights of his sports car had blinked around the corner of the drive.

Seb had given her little boy something that meant a great deal to him.

'Did Seb give you that yesterday? When he came to say goodbye?'

Dan nodded twice, then hesitated for a moment and then his words gushed out in a great rush. 'He said that his grandma gave it to him when he had to leave and go all the way to where the kangaroos live. It kept him safe when he got scared, but now he doesn't need it any more.'

Wide dark amber eyes looked up at her with such love and Ella struggled to keep in control.

'In the night I got scared about the dark and the torch was downstairs and then I put this on my neck and I felt better. I didn't get scared any more. Can I wear it all the time, Mummy? Can I?'

'Of course. Here. Let me fasten it around your neck for you. That was very kind of Seb, wasn't it? Because now you are ready for anything! Taxis. Fast trains! Meeting up with all of your Spanish cousins.'

She hugged Dan closer for a moment before sitting back and pretending to straighten the St Christopher on the front of his T-shirt.

'Grandma and Grandpa are so looking forward to seeing you again. It's been such a long time since Christmas. And you know so many Spanish words; they are going to be so impressed!'

'I'm a bit scared about being there without you, Mummy.'

Me too.

'And what if Milou forgets about me?'

'Hey! Are you forgetting about the magic computer camera that Seb showed you yesterday? Well, there is one for Grandpa, so that I can talk to you and watch you on Grandpa's computer, and Milou can see you too, every day. I promise. Okay? It's only two weeks. Then we have the whole summer to have the best fun together. Isn't that wonderful? Maybe Grandma and Grandpa Martinez could come and visit us here? Then you could show them your room and your school and everything. How's that for an idea?'

He thought about it for a few seconds then nodded furiously, his interest sparked.

'Okay. Do you remember what Nana Bailey says?' Ella asked.

'Time to get the show on the road?'

'That's right! Let's get ready to go on the road. Hands washed!'

Ella helped Dan to his feet and watched him stroke Milou a couple of times before he walked slowly inside, dragging his feet. Milou wagged his tail in delight as Ella rubbed the special point on his ears.

'I did not think it would ever be this hard. It hurts so much without Seb. So very much. I'm going to have to survive without him, but I don't just know how I'm going to do it.'

CHAPTER TWELVE

THE hot afternoon sunshine bounced back from the rippling azure Mediterranean Sea and the shiny polished chrome trim on the stunning white luxury yacht.

Seb caught his tanned but haggard reflection in the mirror-like glass of the main cabin window and ran both hands back through his hair.

So this was what a billionaire looked like.

He had worked all his life for this. It was the crowning achievement the like of which he could not even have dared to dream of as a boy growing up in the Languedoc.

The negotiations had lasted all of Monday and well into the night, but the deal had finally gone through. In two days, Castellano Tech would be part of PSN Media, and every one of his own employees had been guaranteed work or an amazingly generous early retirement package if they wanted it.

And he was going to become the youngest member of the PSN Media Board of Directors with the salary, status, shares and perks to match.

More. The Helene Castellano Foundation had just become a reality.

Shame that he had never felt so lost and miserable in his life.

He missed Ella and Dan so much it hurt. Perhaps that was

why he had worked so feverishly all night to block out any other thoughts except work.

He had never needed people before.

Ella should be standing on this yacht right now helping him celebrate, not clean-shaven men in smart suits popping fine champagne while Matt checked that the lawyers had printed out the final contracts for him to sign.

A massive press conference with television interviews was planned for the afternoon followed by an executive party on the yacht for the new management team.

Ella was the one he wanted to share his excitement and passion. Share his life. Share his future.

It had not taken him long to realise that of course he had been kidding himself. He *had* expected Ella to sacrifice her friends and the pretend family she had created for herself and Dan and replace it with what? A lovely home with everything she could possibly want in education and facilities for Dan. And not one person Dan could call family. Grandparents on the other end of an Internet connection did not play football or come over for birthday parties.

He had wanted her to make all of the sacrifices and compress her life force into a pretty cage he had created for her, while he didn't change a thing.

Ella deserved better than that no matter how much he loved her.

Love? Where had that come from?

His breath caught in his throat as the realisation of what he had done crushed down on top of him with a heavy weight.

He was in love with Ella Jayne Bailey and he loved her precious boy as though he were his own son. Luc Castellano had taught him that it was possible for a man to love someone else's son but he had never imagined knowing how that felt firsthand. Until now.

The thought terrified him, excited him, filled his heart and head with so much light and joy that he should be floating right now.

But he had never told Ella how much he truly cared and how very special she was.

He had come close the night he gave Dan his St Christopher, but had not dared take the final step and make promises to a little boy and his mother he did not know that he could keep.

He would never do that.

So overall he had been a complete idiot.

Suddenly he was aware that Matt was nudging him and Frank Smith, CEO of PSN Media, was looking up from the long glass table, pen in hand.

In an instant he accepted the pen from Frank's hand, scribbled his name in three places, and slapped his new boss on the shoulder.

'Sorry, mates. Have to go. I'm late for a date.'

Ella peered over the dashboard of the very solid and safe estate car her parents-in-law had bought for her within hours of her telling them that she was finally ready to drive again, and tried not to scratch the paintwork on the bushes that lined the familiar lane from the road down to Mas Tournesol.

She had missed this lane so much it felt as though she had been away for two weeks instead of two days.

It was worth the trauma of getting behind the wheel again to be able to drive home to the house she loved so passionately, and the man she knew she was destined to be with.

She was not going to lose Sebastien. And if that meant fighting for him, then so be it. He had filled her dreams and thoughts from the moment they parted and all she longed for was to be with him again.

A familiar bark echoed along the lane and she slowed the car down to a halt. Some things had not changed!

Milou was lying in the road in his favourite spot, stretched out in the sunshine and yawning widely, then wagging his tail as fast as he could muster as soon as he recognised her.

Ella had just bent down to stroke his head when a familiar very red but rather dented sports car raced up the lane from the house and screeched to a stop just short of Milou's tail.

Seb jumped out and walked the few steps towards her before snatching off his sunglasses and gazing at her as though he could not believe his eyes.

They both stood in stunned silence for a few seconds, her heart racing in tune with his breathing, and then he smiled and lowered his hands to his hips.

'I'm sorry, *mademoiselle*, but Milou does not speak English. Can I help you?'

His lower lip was quivering so hard as he fought to contain his laughter that she relaxed enough to pick up on the joke. Anything to ease the heartache of simply seeing his face again.

'Hello.' She swallowed hard. 'I'm looking for the Sunflower House. Am I on the right road?'

'Just carry on. It's the end of the lane. Miss?'

'Bailey. Ella Jayne Bailey.'

'Hello, Miss Ella Jayne Bailey,' he answered with a smile. They grinned at each other for a second.

'Is Nicole here?' she asked tentatively.

'Just arrived.' His hand slid across the side of her car as he stepped closer. 'Nice wheels. Do they do it in red?'

Her eyes never left his smiling face as she replied.

'A present from Dan's grandparents.' And then the intensity of his smile burnt through her hesitation and she shuffled one step nearer. 'Is everything okay?'

Are you okay?

There was a low gravelly sigh. 'I collected Nicole from

the airport. And we talked. Really talked. I was on my way to Barcelona to convince you to change your mind.'

Ella shook her head. 'I was on my way back from Barcelona to persuade you to change your mind. But I don't understand. What made you reconsider?'

'André Morel let the most precious people in his life slip away from him because he was too scared—scared of settling down as a husband. Scared of taking the responsibility. I'm not repeating that same mistake.'

Seb reached into the pocket of his denims and pulled out a familiar set of long ornate keys, and he moved a few steps closer, so that his other hand was only inches from Ella's.

Her head lifted and she focused on his face.

'Nicole is building a new life for herself in Paris and London, so I made her an offer she couldn't refuse, with the promise of a warm welcome any time she liked.'

Seb lowered the keys into the palm of Ella's hand and slowly closed her fingers around them.

'Nicole sold you the house?'

'This is the home I always wanted to come back to. If I am honest, I carried it with me every step of the journey back here. Now I know that I couldn't live anywhere else in the world.'

'Why? Tell me.'

'Because you are here.'

Seb's hands came up slowly to support her face, his long fingers tenderly caressing her skin as he leant in towards her, his deep brown eyes burrowing into hers as their bodies touched.

Ella could feel his warm breath on her skin as he whispered the words she had longed to hear, his voice low and trembling.

'I need you, Ella. I love you and I love Dan as though he was my own son. I can work *anywhere*. Go *anywhere*. And if you feel the same I'm happy to make my home right here. Just say the word. Are you willing to give us a chance for happiness together?'

Ella pressed her lips gently against his, desperate to reassure him. 'I am. More than ever. I never thought that I would feel this way again, Seb. I love you. I love you and I want to share your life, no matter where that might take me. You have brought me so much happiness in these last few days.'

His broad grin made her heart sing. 'This is a first for me. You hit me hard, Ella Jayne, and I'm still reeling. I don't want to lose you, Ella. You or Dan.'

His forehead pressed against hers. 'I have a new job. There will still be some travelling, but I can make sure that the dates match up with weekends and school holidays and we can make them family trips.'

His voice trembled with excitement and happiness. 'Can you imagine taking Dan into the jungle or swimming on the Great Barrier Reef? Seeing kangaroos in the wild for the first time? And he would be meeting some great kids from all walks of life on the way. I'd love to have you both with me!'

She laughed out loud and grinned at him, crazy with wild emotion. 'Dan and kangaroos! You might have to buy a farm for all of his new pets.'

His hand moved behind Ella's head so that he could whisper the words.

'Then be with me, Ella, and make my house a home again. We might even have a party to celebrate. Starting today.'

Coming Next Month

Available April 12, 2011

#4231 THE BABY PROJECT
Susan Meier
Babies in the Boardroom

#4232 IN THE AUSTRALIAN BILLIONAIRE'S ARMS
Margaret Way

#4233 HOW TO LASSO A COWBOY
Shirley Jump
The Fun Factor

#4234 RICHES TO RAGS BRIDE
Myrna Mackenzie

#4235 RANCHER'S TWINS: MOM NEEDED
Barbara Hannay
Rugged Ranchers

#4236 FRIENDS TO FOREVER
Nikki Logan

HRCNM0311

Selene wanted nothing to do with the father of her son, Alex; but Aristedes had other plans...that included them.

Read on for an sneak peek from THE SARANTOS SECRET BABY by Olivia Gates, available April 2011, only from Harlequin Desire.

"You were right to turn my marriage offer down," Aristedes said.

And Selene found her voice at last, found the words that would not betray the blow he'd dealt her. "Thanks for letting me know. You didn't have to come all the way here, though. You could have just let it go. I left yesterday with the understanding that this case is closed."

Before the hot needles behind her eyes could dissolve into an unforgivable display of stupidity and weakness, she began to close the door.

The door stopped against an immovable object. His flat palm.

"I can't accept that." His voice was low, leashed.

What did her tormentor mean now? Was he ending one game only to start another?

She raised eyes as bruised as her self-respect to his, found nothing there but solemnity and determination.

Before she could voice her confusion, he elaborated. "I never let anything go unless I'm certain it's unworkable. I realize I made you an unworkable offer, and that's why I'm withdrawing it. I'm here to offer something else. A workability study."

She leaned against the door, thankful for its support and partial shield. "Your son and I are not a business venture you can test for feasibility."

His gaze grew deeper, made her feel as if he was trying to delve into her mind, take control of it. "It's actually the

SDEXP0411

other way around. I'm the one who would be tested."

She shook her head. "Why bother? I know—and *you* know—you're not workable. Not with me."

His spectacular eyebrows lowered over eyes she felt were emitting silver hypnosis. "You're right again. Neither you nor I have any reason to believe that isn't the truth. The only truth. It might be best for both you and Alex to never hear from me again, to forget I exist. But then again, maybe not. I'm only asking for the chance for both of us to find out for certain. You believe I'm unworkable in any personal relationship. I've lived my life based on that belief about myself. I never really had reason to question it. But I have one now. In fact, I have two."

Find out what happens in
THE SARANTOS SECRET BABY by Olivia Gates,
available April 2011, only from Harlequin Desire.

SDEXP0411